SLAUGHTER IN TEXAS
THE CROCKETTS' WESTERN SAGA: 2

ROBERT VAUGHAN

WOLFPACK
PUBLISHING
— EST 2013 —

WOLFPACK
PUBLISHING
— EST 2013 —

Published in the United States by Wolfpack Publishing, Las Vegas

Wolfpack Publishing
5130 S. Fort Apache Road, 215-380
Las Vegas, NV 89148

wolfpackpublishing.com

Paperback ISBN 978-1-64734-722-2
eBook ISBN 978-1-64734-721-5

SLAUGHTER IN TEXAS

Chapter One

Will and Gideon Crockett were in Southwest Texas, having arrived there in a casual westward drift that neither proposed a particular destination nor had a sense of purpose. The brothers hailed from Missouri, but years of bloody border war as members of Quantrill's Raiders had set them on their wandering. They were called Bushwhackers then and still thought of themselves in such terms. Their wartime activity had earned them a degree of notoriety and, like Frank and Jesse James, the Younger brothers, and others who had ridden with them during the late war, they were now regarded as outlaws and their pictures could occasionally be found on old reward posters in Missouri, Kansas, Arkansas, Louisiana, and even parts of Texas.

At the end of the Civil War, millions of soldiers who had worn the blue and the gray laid down their arms and picked up where they had left off. Friendships were renewed, crops were put in, men and women were married, children were born, and their lives went on as if nothing had happened.

But it was not to be so for all men. For some, the wounds had cut too deeply, and the price had been too dear. Families, fortunes, and dreams were consumed in flames and drowned in blood.

Will and Gideon Crockett were such men. They had only each other, a dwindling number of their peers, their guns, their courage, and a peculiar though quite rigid code of honor to sustain them. For them the war had not ended. Only the battles had changed.

For some after the last cannon had fired, their last rifle put down, men drifted around without purpose or destination. Generally, the Crockett brothers fit that description.

But not now, though, Will and Gid were headed for Shafter, Texas, because it was said that silver had been discovered there, and like thousands before them, it was time to seek their fortune.

The closest railroad stop to Shafter was Marfa, Texas. Gid's first impression of Marfa, was one of incredible heat. It bore down on him like some great weight. He stood on the station platform while behind him vented steam from the train's escape valve sounded like some exhausted monster, gasping for breath in the terrible heat. Heat waves shimmered up from the streets and Gid wondered what kept the town from just melting.

Will had gone forward to check on the horses that had ridden in the stock car.

Gid saw a black frying pan sitting on a stump and he walked over and picked it up. The handle of the skillet was as hot as if it had been sitting over an open fire, and with a sharp exclamation of pain he dropped the pan.

There were three or four of the town's citizens were sitting on a baggage cart under the shade of the car shed's overhang. When they saw Gid's reaction, they all burst out in loud guffaws.

"Was the pan hot, mister?" one of them asked.

"Not really," Gid answered, managing a good-natured grin despite his embarrassment.

"It wasn't? Why, you sure put it down fast," another of the men said.

"Well, hell, how long does it take to look at a pan?" Gid asked.

"How long does it take to look at a pan?" the man replied, and he and the others laughed loudly at Gid's rejoinder. "That's pretty good. We've caught lots of folks with that skillet, but you been the best yet. Mister, you're all right in our book."

"Why do you keep this skillet sitting out here like

this?" Gid asked.

"Well, since you been such a good sport about it, I'll tell you the truth," one of the men said. "We're trollin' for fools."

"What?"

"You got any idea how hot a black iron skillet like that can get in this sun? Well, you do now, you picked it up. But there's lots of folks who are just as curious, and if you'll excuse me for sayin' so, just as much a fool as you were. They can't keep their hands offen it. They walk over and pick it up, and we get our little laugh. Like I say, we're trollin' for fools."

"Let me show you somethin', mister," one of the others said. He picked up an egg and brought it over to the pan, then broke it. The egg began to sizzle and turn white.

Gid chuckled. "There must not be a hell of a lot to do in Marfa if you have to stay down here and do this," he said.

"Oh, I wouldn't say that. Problem is that the town don't really come to life 'till it's dark.

Will came up to join his brother.

"The horses made the trip just fine," he said.

"Where are they?"

"I've already made a deal to have them put up at the corral." He saw Gid holding his hand. "What happened to your hand?"

"Nothin'. Hey, Will, do you see that skillet over there,

sittin' on the stump?" Gid asked.

Will glanced over. "Yeah, I see it. What about it?"

"Looks like a pretty good skillet to me. Someone must've left it there. Why don't you go get it?"

"That would be a damn fool thing to do, don't you think? I mean, to pick up a black iron skillet that's been sittin' in the sun all day."

Gid looked over at the men who had caught him with the trick, and they smiled at him.

"Yeah," Gid said, still rubbing his hand. "Yeah, that would be pretty much of a fool thing to do, all right."

Although he was the older of the two brothers, Will was the smaller. He was about five feet, eight inches tall, with ash-blond hair and the hard face and seasoned blue eyes of someone who had seen more than his share of hard times. Gid was six foot one, with broad shoulders, and darker hair. Anyone could see that Gid was Will's brother, if they happened to look into his eyes. They were the duplicate of Will's, and they measured life with the same reserved scrutiny. But there the similarity stopped. Gid was a powerful man whose first solution to any problem was his strength. Will had a wiry toughness about him, but his greatest strength was in his wits and quickness. Both men made formidable enemies, and neither was a stranger to the gun, should the situation reach that extreme.

Leaving the depot, the two brothers walked to the nearest saloon.

"Let's go in and get us a couple of beers," Will said. "We'll find some supper and then get a room for the night. We can head out for Shafter tomorrow morning."

"Damn, that's a forty-mile ride going south. Why don't we stay here and see what Marfa has to offer? Gid questioned.

"Look around this town," Will said. "Do you see anything for us to do? Or do you want to join those old codgers who sit around trying to trick newcomers into picking up a hot skillet?"

Gid turned his hand over, the redness still very much visible. "I guess not. We came out here to prospect for silver and we can't let a little heat stop us."

"Then we'll get an early start in the morning when it won't be so hot."

Six hours after leaving Marfa, the brothers rode into Shafter.

Shafter was laid out in neat squares, with the streets and the houses baking under the sun. Main Street had several places of business—a couple of general stores, two hotels, an apothecary, a freight office, a building that bore the sign Presidio Silver Mining Company, and three saloons. One third of the town occupying the south side was obviously Mexican, as identified by the Spanish language signs and the adobe buildings.

Making arrangements with a livery to board their horses, the two brothers walked up the wide, sunbaked street, hurrying from the shade of one adobe building to the next, taking every opportunity to get out of the sun. After a walk of a few blocks they were drenched with sweat, and the cool interior of the Dust Cutter Saloon beckoned them. A sign outside the saloon promised cold beer and they thought nothing could be better than that. They pushed their way through the bat wing doors and went inside. It was so dark that they had to stand there for a moment or two until their eyes adjusted. The bar was made of burnished mahogany with a highly polished brass footrail. Crisp, clean white towels hung from hooks on the customers' side of the bar, spaced every four feet. A mirror behind the bar was flanked on each side by a small statue of a nude woman set back in a special niche. A row of whiskey bottles sat in front of the mirror, reflected in the glass so that the row of bottles seemed to be two deep. A bartender with pomaded black hair and a waxed handlebar moustache stood behind the bar industriously polishing glasses.

"Is the beer really cold?" Gid asked.

The bartender looked up at him, but he didn't stop polishing the glasses. "It's cooler than horse piss," he said, in a matter-of-fact voice.

"Two beers," Will said.

"And I'll have the same," Gid added. The bartender, who thought that Will had ordered for both of them, chuckled, then drew the beers and put them in front of the two brothers.

Will picked up the first beer and took a long drink before he turned to look around the place. A card game was going on in the corner and he watched it for a few minutes while he drank his beer.

The back door opened and a tall, broad-shouldered, bearded man wearing a badge stepped inside. He pointed a gun toward the table.

"Bell, I didn't think you'd be dumb enough to come back to Shafter."

The man the marshal was talking to, one of the card players, stood up slowly, then turned to face the marshal.

"Yeah, well, I decided not to let any pissant of a marshal run me out."

The situation had the look of an impending gunfight, and the remaining card players jumped up from the table and moved out of the way.

"I gave you two choices, get out of town or spend time in my jail. Looks to me like you've made your choice," the marshal said.

"I wouldn't want to be goin' to jail," Bell said. "Not

with this here winnin' hand I got."

"Unbuckle your gun belt, slow and easy," the marshal ordered.

Bell shook his head. "I don't think so, Vidal. I think me an' you are goin' to have to settle this thing, once and for all."

Will, like the others, was watching the drama unfold, when he heard something, a soft squeaking sound as if weight were being put down on a loose board. He looked up toward the top of the stairs and saw a man standing there, aiming a shotgun at the marshal's back.

"Marshal, look out!" Will shouted. When he shouted the warning, the man wielding the shotgun turned it toward Will and Gid.

"You squealin' son of a bitch!" he shouted. The shotgun boomed loudly.

Will had no choice then. He dropped his beer and pulled his pistol, firing just as the man at the top of the stairs squeezed his own trigger. Will and Gid had jumped in opposite directions just as the man fired. The heavy charge of buckshot tore a large hole in the top and side of the bar, right where the two brothers had been standing. Some of the shot hit the whiskey bottles, the mirror, and one of the nude statues behind the bar. Like shrapnel from an exploding bomb, pieces of glass flew everywhere. The mirror fell, except for a few jagged shards that hung in place where the mirror had been, reflecting twisting images of the dramatic scene before it.

Will's shot had been accurately placed; the man with the shotgun dropped his weapon and grabbed his neck. He stood there, stupidly, for a moment, clutching his neck as blood spilled between his fingers. Then his eyes rolled up in his head and he fell, twisting around so that, on his back and head-first, he slid down the stairs, following his clattering shotgun to the ground floor. He lay motionless with open, sightless eyes staring up toward the ceiling.

The sound of the two gunshots had riveted everyone's attention to that exchange, and while their attention was diverted from him, Bell took the opportunity to go for his own gun. Suddenly the saloon was filled with the roar of another gunshot as Bell fired at Marshal Vidal.

Vidal had made the mistake of being diverted by the gunplay between Will and the shotgun shooter. It was a fatal mistake, because Bell's bullet struck the marshal in the forehead and the impact knocked him back onto a nearby table. Vidal lay belly up on the table with his head hanging down on the far side while blood dripped from the hole in his forehead to form a puddle below him. His gun fell from his lifeless hand and clattered to the floor. Bell then swung his pistol toward Will. For a moment the two men stood *en tableau*, each holding a gun on the other.

"Mister, this ain't my fight," Will said.

"Wrong. You made it your fight when you kilt my pardner. Now I reckon I'm goin' to have to kill you."

While Bell was talking, Will was acting. He pulled the trigger and his bullet caught Bell in the center of his chest. Bell went down, dead before he hit the floor.

"What's goin' on in here?" a voice asked. "What's all the shootin'?"

When Will turned toward the sound of the voice, he saw a man standing just inside the open door. Because of the brightness of the light behind the man Will couldn't make out his features.

"Get out of the light," Will growled.

"You don't tell me what to do, I—"

Will pulled the hammer back and his pistol made a deadly metallic click as the sear engaged the cylinder.

"Get out of the light or I'll kill you where you stand."

The figure moved out of the light. When he did, Will saw that he was wearing a sheriff's badge. He put his pistol away.

"Sheriff, I'm glad you come," one of the men who had been playing cards said. "This here fella just shot Ernest Fowler and Leo Bell down in cold blood."

"You lying son of a bitch," Will said. "I don't know who you are but—"

"That's Roscoe Gentry," the sheriff said. "He's my

deputy. And if he says you kilt them two men then I'm goin' to have to take you in."

Although Will had already holstered his pistol, it suddenly appeared in his hand again, the draw as fast as the wink of an eye.

"I don't think so, Sheriff," Will said. By now, Gid had his gun out as well and between the two of them, everyone in the saloon was effectively covered. "Now, I don't know what this man saw, or thinks he saw. But the man lying belly up on the table over there is a lawman. I didn't have anything to do with killing him. The other two were trying to kill me."

"Sheriff Jones, Gentry is the one who is lying," one of the other saloon patrons said. "This fella is telling the truth. Ernest Fowler started shootin' first, usin' a scatter gun. Take a look at the bar there and you'll see what I'm talkin' about. Then Bell killed Vidal and swung his gun around toward this fella, tellin' him he was fixin' to kill him too. Knowin' Bell, you got to figure that he was goin' to do just what he said. For a minute there, they had what you might call a Mexican standoff. Then, this fella pulled the trigger ... which if you ask me, he had every right to do."

"Why should I listen to you, Rankin?" Jones asked. "Bell and Fowler both rode for the McAfees and ever' one knows you ain't been none too friendly with the McAfees. And if memory serves me, you had a run-in with Bell over

12

a few head of cows not long ago."

"I still believe the son of a bitch meant to steal those cows," Rankin replied. "But that has nothing to do with what happened here. I'm telling you the truth about what I saw."

"Dan ain't lying, sheriff," the bartender said. "Except for Roscoe Gentry, you can ask anyone in here, they'll all say the same thing."

There was a general buzz of agreement from all the other patrons in the saloon.

Sheriff Jones glared at Dan Rankin for a moment more, then he pointed at Will. "All right, I got nothing on you now," he said. "But I'll be keepin' my eye on you." He turned and walked out.

"Sheriff, wait!" Gentry called. Looking cautiously at Will and Gid, all the while holding his hands up to show that he represented no danger to them, Gentry hurried to join Sheriff Jones in making an exit.

"I'll be damned," Will said after Gentry and the sheriff left. "They didn't seem at all concerned that another lawman was killed."

"Sheriff Jones and Deputy Gentry wasn't exactly what you'd call friendly with Marshal Vidal," the bartender explained. He drew two more beers. "My name is Henry. Henry Deer. And these are on the house," he said, sliding them across to the two brothers.

"Thanks, Henry," Will said. He looked at the young cowboy who had backed him up. "And I want to thank you, too, Rankin, for telling the sheriff how it was."

"Think nothin' of it," Rankin said. "Truth to tell, you prob'ly made yourself a lot of friends around here, today."

"How's that?" Will asked.

Rankin nodded toward the bodies, which were now being carried out of the saloon.

"Marshal Vidal was a good man. If it had been up to Sheriff Jones and Deputy Gentry, he would've been shot down today, and nothing would have happened to the two who did it. I reckon the town folk are all goin' to figure justice was served."

"Why don't you tell him the rest of it, Rankin?" Henry asked.

"Yeah, well, when word gets around about what happened, you'll wind up having made yourself as many enemies as you have friends," Rankin said. "And the enemies you'll make—Moe Tucker, Isaac and Amos McAfee—aren't the kind of enemies a man wants to have."

"Who are they?" Will asked.

"They're ranchers," Rankin answered. "And they're dangerous men to cross."

"You see, boys," Henry continued, "what you have stumbled into is sort of a war."

"A war?"

"Yes, with the ranchers and the cowboys on one side, and the miners and the townspeople on the other side."

"But you're a rancher, aren't you?" Will asked Dan. "Which side are you on?"

"I'm on Dan Rankin's side," Dan answered, easily.

Chapter Two

For J.C. Malone, the editor of the Shafter newspaper which was called *The Bi-Weekly Defender,* Will and Gid Crockett's' arrival in town occurred at exactly the right time. He was just putting the day's newspaper together and what had been the lead, a story about a new smelter being installed in the Mina Grande Mine, was replaced with a story of the gunfight.

YESTERDAY'S FATEFUL EVENTS

Three Men Hurled Into Eternity

In The Blink Of An Eye

In the story that followed, the editor of *The Bi-Weekly Defender* left no doubt as to where he stood. Although all good men of the town would lament the passing of Marshal Vidal, there would be no tears shed over the deaths of Ernest Fowler and Leo Bell.

Seven miles from town, along the Cibolo Creek, Moe Tucker heard Sheriff Jones and Deputy Gentry's account of what had happened.

"Was this fella that good? Or was he just lucky?" Moe asked. He and his younger brother, Lenny, owned the Tucker ranch, the largest of all the area ranches. Lenny Tucker wasn't present for this particular discussion, but Moe's neighbors and closest friends, Isaac and Amos McAfee were. The McAfee brothers owned the adjoining ranch.

"I couldn't say he was all that good," Gentry said, answering the question. "The thing is, Ernest wasn't expectin' a stranger to take a hand in a private fight. And then, when the stranger killed Leo, he already had the drop on him. I seen that myself. He just up and pulled the trigger."

"Why didn't you take a hand in it?" Moe asked. "You was there."

"Yeah, well, the thing is, I didn't have no idea none of this was goin' to happen neither. First thing you know there was all this shootin' goin' on, and the next thing you know, this here stranger was standin' there holdin' a gun in his hand. What was I supposed to do?" Gentry said, defending himself.

"Who are they, anyhow?"

"I don't know, I never seen any one of 'em before. Him and his brother just come into town, yesterday. I talked to some people who seen 'em get off the train."

"I don't like havin' people like that around," Moe said. "You're goin' to have to get rid of 'em, some way."

"Maybe there'll be no need for that," Gentry suggested. "Could be they'll move on by them ownselves if we just wait."

"If?" Moe asked, glaring at him. "If a frog had wings, he wouldn't bump his ass ever' time he jumps," he said. "We got things goin' our way aroun' here and it'll keep on goin' our way 'long as the people in town don't get a backbone. I don't want these two men givin' 'em that backbone."

Two miles away from the house, Lenny Tucker swung down from his horse and walked over to the edge of the cliff to look down into the canyon below. He was short and slim, with sandy hair and blue eyes. He wasn't wearing a gun belt, though he did have a rifle in a saddle scabbard.

The horse was pulling at the reins, trying to get to some grass, so Lenny dropped them to let him nibble around the few sweet green shoots he was able to find on the rocky ledge.

"So, what do you think, Dancer? You want to go into town tonight?"

The horse chewed loudly.

"Don't talk with your mouth full," Lenny teased. He walked over and patted Dancer affectionately on the neck. "Too bad they don't have any mares boarded at the Jingle Bob Corral," he said. "If they did, you could have some fun there while I'm over at the Carnation House. I ought to tell Muley that. He could get some brood mares brought in, and the Jingle Bob Corral could become a whore house for horses." He laughed out loud. "Yeah," he said. "I like that idea. A whorehouse for horses."

Lenny swung into the saddle and started back toward the house. He had heard Moe say earlier that he was going into town also. He just hoped that Moe would stay out of trouble tonight. He loved his brother, but Moe was very hot tempered, and when he got drunk, which was often, he could be a major pain in the ass.

Although the Tucker Ranch, the Double T, and the McAfee Ranch, the Bar M Bar, were the two biggest ranches in the county, theirs weren't the only ranches. There were at least half-a-dozen others, including the Rankin spread. Dan Rankin, who once rode for Moe and Lenny Tucker, had realized the dream of every cowboy by starting his own ranch. A small ranch as local ranches went, it was wedged in, like a piece of pie between the Tucker place and the McAfee spread. The large end of the pie-shaped wedge was bordered by the river. And, while the river frontage made Dan's ranch feasible, that same frontage was also a thorn in Moe Tucker's side. Moe reasoned that he could increase the size of his herd by twenty-five percent if he had the river frontage that now belonged to Dan Rankin.

What made Dan's possession of the land even more difficult for Moe Tucker to swallow was the fact that the land had once been Tucker land. He and Lenny had given it to their sister, Hilda, so she could build a house there, when she got married.

But Hilda was a homely woman who, even with her land, was unable to catch the eye of a suitor. And although Dan never actually paid court to Hilda, he did treat her kindly and Hilda remembered that. When she died of some undiagnosed malady, Moe, Lenny, and, most of all Dan were surprised to discover that Hilda Tucker had left her land and all her possessions to Dan Rankin.

Lenny had passed it off, saying that it had been Hilda's land to do with as she saw fit, but Moe was angry about it and went to a lawyer to try and break the will. There was nothing he could do to break the will as it stood, but there was a codicil to Hilda's will that stated that Dan Rankin must work the ranch for ten consecutive years, or the land would return to her brothers.

In one day, Dan Rankin went from being a rider for Moe Tucker to the biggest thorn in his side. It was not a situation Moe accepted easily; he did everything he could to make it difficult for Dan, hoping to force him off before he had fulfilled the ten years required by the will.

To that end, he let it be known that any cowboy who rode for Dan would never again be able to ride for him. He undersold Dan in the cattle market, and he booked more cattle cars than he needed, thus denying Dan rail transportation. He also let his cattle graze on Dan's land and urged Isaac and Amos McAfee to do the same thing in order to thin Dan's grass.

Because Dan was the smallest rancher in the county, in terms of acreage and size of herd, he did not feel that the ranchers' dispute with the townspeople had anything to do with him. But, because he was a rancher and not a town merchant, neither did he ally himself with the town. The result was that in the quarrel between the ranchers and the town, Dan neither took a side nor did he have an ally.

On the Rankin Ranch, Dan sat on a stone outcrop and leaned back against a boulder. Though literally as hard as a rock, the seat felt comfortable to him because it was the first time he had been off a horse in several hours. His legs hurt and his seat was sore, and he was so tired he could stretch out right here and go to sleep.

Slim, his foreman, brought him a skillet of beans and bacon. There were a couple of biscuits and an onion slice on the side.

"Uhmm, biscuits? Dan said.

"They can't no one make biscuits to compare with Slim's, not even that Mex cook Marie Lacoste has at that fancy whorehouse she runs," Underhill, one of the drovers, said. "Boss, I tell you, Slim is gonna make some hard-drivin' woman an awful good husband," he teased. "Hell, come to think of it, I might even marry him my own self."

Underhill and the others guffawed and Slim, who was emptying the last dregs of a cup of coffee, threw the rest toward the man who was teasing him. It was all in good fun, though, with little chance of an actual fight erupting. There were four men sitting around the fire and two more out riding night herd. Those six represented Dan's entire outfit. The fire had just about burned down and was little more than glowing embers.

"Boss, I throwed your roll down over here," Levi said. Nearly sixty, Levi was by far the oldest of the drovers and was sort of the father figure to all of them. "It's on high ground 'n' 'bout as level as anyplace I could find around here."

"Thanks, Levi," Dan said as he raked his biscuit through the last of the bean juice. He dunked his kit in a bucket of water, cleaned it off with some sand, then folded it and put it away.

The other men had all ridden for other spreads before they came to work for Dan. Dan wasn't able to pay them the same wages the other ranchers could, but he offered them something more. He offered them a share in the herd. He would keep the land for his own, but he promised his cowboys that they would share in ownership of the herd. That arrangement had created binding loyalties and strengthened friendships. Dan's ranch might be the smallest in the county, he reasoned, but everyone who worked there believed it was, by far, the best place to be.

When the men who worked for Dan encountered the hands from the other ranches in town, they sometimes teased them for being *cowboys,* while they, by virtue of their joint ownership of the herd, were *cattlemen.* It made for some lively discussions at the Dust Cutter Saloon and the Carnation House.

The Carnation House was a large, two-story Victorian house that stood just on the edge of Shafter. It was surrounded by a lawn kept green by irrigation, as well as a few mimosa trees. It was, in fact, the handsomest house in all of town.

Ten young women called Carnation House home, and for more than half of them it was the best home they had ever had. Many of the girls had been raised as orphans or had been in abusive relationships.

Now they regarded each other as sisters rather than co-workers. They could gather in a parlor where convivial conversations took place, they had three good meals a day and each had a private room with curtains on the windows and a wardrobe for their clothes. They also had a comfortable bed in which they were able to sleep.

Sometimes, for according to who was telling the story, they were called soiled doves, ladies of the evening, fallen women, or prostitutes.

Lucy Briggs, one of the girls of Carnation House, was in the parlor, sitting on the sofa with her legs drawn up under her, reading the paper.

"Señorita Lucy, would you like a cup of coffee?" the cook asked.

Lucy smiled at him, sweetly. "Oh, yes, Munoz, that would be wonderful, thank you."

"What have you found in the paper that is so interesting?" Marie Lacoste asked. Marie was the madam of the house, and though she wasn't much older than the girls who worked there, they looked upon her almost as much as a mother, as they did a boss.

"It's a story about the shooting in the Dust Cutter," Lucy said.

"Why do you have to read about it? My goodness, didn't I tell you what happened?" one of the girls said. "I was there."

"Yes, but almost everyone who came in last night had a different story to tell. If you read it in the paper, you can count on Mr. Malone to tell you the real truth."

"Well, heavens, Susie, are you saying you can't depend on what Lenny had to say? You and Lenny are as tight as two peas in the pod. You know he won't see any girl but you when he comes in here."

"I asked him last night, but he said he didn't want to talk about it."

"Your coffee, Señorita," Munoz said, bringing a steaming cup.

"*Gracias, Señor Munoz,*" Lucy replied with a broad smile.

"Deputy Gentry lied, trying to get the two strangers in trouble," Lucy said. "It's a shame ..." she grew quiet, leaving her sentence unfinished.

"You can say it. It's a shame Gentry wasn't one of the ones who was killed," Marie said.

Lucy laughed. "Oh, is it evil of me to think such a thing?"

"Since when is it evil to put a stop to evil? Roscoe Gentry is the most despicable man God has ever put on this earth. Why in heaven's name He did that is certainly a mystery to me."

The grandfather clock that sat against the wall whirred, then struck six times, the melodious chimes echoing throughout the downstairs of Carnation House.

Lucy lay the paper aside then stood. "I'd better go upstairs and get ready," she said.

Marie watched as Lucy started up the wide staircase. Marie was most discriminating in her hiring, choosing only those girls that she personally liked.

"You're going to find many in this town who will not treat you kindly," *Marie had told each of the girls as they joined the group.* "So, we will have to be a family. Just as it's important that I like you, it is equally important that you like one another."

Marie tried to have the same feelings for all of the girls, but she couldn't help but like Lucy the best.

It didn't take Gid Crockett long to discover the Carnation House. Billing itself as a "Sporting House for Gentlemen," its owner, Marie Lacoste, even advertised her services in The Bi-Weekly Defender:

The Carnation House

a

Sporting House for Gentlemen

Where

Beautiful and Cultured

Ladies

Will provide you with every

Pleasure

When Gid reached the big, white, two story house he hesitated for a moment. The advertisement in the newspaper had called the Carnation House a "sporting house for gentlemen" and in Gid's lexicon, that meant it was a house of prostitution. He had never seen a whorehouse as wholesome looking as this one appeared to be.

He was even more uncertain when he stepped inside. He was in a grand foyer that opened onto a large parlor where he saw elegant furniture, beautiful paintings, and posh draperies—not unlike what might be found in a wealthy man's mansion.

Several young women were sitting in the parlor, all of them dressed as if they were going to the latest meeting of the sewing circle.

Gid was confused and turned to go.

"Welcome to Carnation House," a very attractive woman said as she stepped into the foyer. She stuck out her hand. "My name's Marie Lacoste."

"I'm Gideon Crockett, though most folks call me Gid. Marie, is this a ... uh ..."

Marie nodded her head.

"I own the place," she said with a welcoming grin. "Why don't you step into the parlor and meet some of the girls?"

"It's him," Gid heard someone say. "He's one o' the

two brothers that was at the Dust Cutter last night. His brother, it was, that shot two of 'em."

"What'd this fella do?"

"Mostly, or at least what it looked like, this here one just sort of backed up his brother. I didn't actually see him doin' hardly nothin' at all 'cept to hold a gun in his hand. But it made Gentry 'n them others back down, I can tell you that for sure."

Marie watched a couple of the girls approach the man who had identified himself as Gideon Crockett. She smiled because she knew that any need he might have would be taken care of.

Marie made no apologies about running a whorehouse.

"Why should I be ashamed of it?" she would reply to anyone who questioned her. "I give my girls a clean place to stay and I insist that the gentlemen callers be on their best behavior. If they are not well behaved, I don't let them return."

Marie had been in town for nearly two years having come to Shafter as a member of a theater group. The owner of the repertoire company for which Marie worked had lost all the box office receipts in an after-show poker game, then tried to take them back at gunpoint. That was a fatal mistake, and he now lay buried out on Boot Hill under a marker which read:

Here lies
LUCIEN THOMPKINS
an actor whose brief hour
upon the stage is no more
his final act ended by
two slugs from a .44

When the rest of the theater company left town, Marie stayed. She was a beautiful woman and her role in the theater had inflamed the fantasies of many men. Marie had only to play upon those fantasies to become a very successful prostitute. It was rumored that she had been the mistress of a Russian Prince during his visit to the American West, and because Marie knew that such rumors fed the fantasies of men who wanted to "do it with a woman who had done it with a prince," she did nothing to dispel the rumors.

When Marie made enough money, she built the Carnation House and hired only the most attractive women she could find. She then went into semiretirement, preferring to manage the affairs of her girls over providing her personal services to the customers.

At the precise moment that Gid was meeting some of the girls of Carnation House, his brother, Will, was down the street playing poker in the Dust Cutter Saloon.

"I'll take three," the man in black said. He put his discards on the table, then began coughing. Taking his handkerchief from his inside jacket pocket, he held it over his mouth until the coughing fit passed. Will noticed that the handkerchief was flecked with blood.

The dealer gave the man in black three cards, then looked over at Will.

"And what about you, sir?" the dealer asked. "How many cards?"

"One," Will said.

"Drawing to an inside straight are you?" the dealer joked, slapping a new card down in front of Will.

Will was actually trying to fill a heart flush, but when he saw that the card was a spade, he folded.

"Well, Doc Hawkins, it's going to cost you five bucks to see what I've got," one of the players said.

Will glanced quickly at the man in black. None of the players had introduced themselves and not until that moment did he know that he was playing with Doc Hawkins. He had never met Doc Hawkins, but he had certainly heard of him.

Doc Hawkins looked at his cards, thought about it for a moment, then folded with a shrug.

One of the other players, who had bet heavily on this hand and lost, pushed his chair back from the table.

"Boys, I'd better give this game up while I still got enough to buy myself a beer," he said.

Just as he was leaving the game, three men were coming into the saloon. One of them, seeing an open chair, came over to the table and, without being asked, sat down. It was fairly obvious that the new player had been drinking pretty heavily.

"A person with manners would have asked if he could join," Doc said.

"I got as much right here as anyone at this table," the man said. "My family's been here long before the town."

"We know all about you, Moe Tucker," the dealer said, "and we know how important your papa was. Are you sure you want to play cards?"

"I'm sittin' here, ain't I?"

"You're also drunk. I don't want you comin' back here tomorrow, complainin' because we took advantage of you while you were drunk."

"What's the matter?" Moe snarled. "You afraid to let me play?"

"Let him play," Doc said. "I've been admiring that hat of his. I might just win it tonight."

Moe took off his hat, a low-crowned, black hat sporting a band of silver conchos.

"You ain't gettin' my hat," he said. He pulled a stack of bills from his pocket and put them on the table in front of him. "On the other hand, after I take all your money, I might just win that fancy vest you're wearin' to go with my hat."

Doc chuckled. "We'll see, Mr. Tucker, we'll see," he said.

By now Will had heard that Moe Tucker was one of the principles in the dispute between the townspeople and the ranchers, so he studied the new player closely. Moe was of medium height and build, with brown hair, clean-shaven, but with a pockmarked face. He also had a broken tooth.

"What are you lookin' at?" Moe snarled when he realized Will had been scrutinizing him.

"I haven't quite figured out what I'm looking at," Will said.

Moe snorted, then played the cards that were dealt him. Will won that hand. He won the next hand as well, and with that hand was now a few dollars ahead.

"You're a pretty lucky fella," Moe said.

"Sometimes it happens," Will said, as he raked in his winnings.

"Yeah, like it happened yesterday. You was lucky then too, wasn't you? I mean, when you killed Bell and Fowler?"

Will looked at him but didn't answer.

"I guess you know they were friends of mine," Moe said. "They were good men, both of 'em. They didn't deserve to be shot down like dogs in the street. Especially by some drifter who just rode into town."

"That's where you are wrong, Tucker," Doc Hawkins said. "They *did* deserve to be shot down like dogs in the street. They were both sorry bastards and I should have killed them myself, a long time ago. And as far as I'm concerned—as far as most of the town is concerned—it was good riddance."

"I ain't talkin' to you, Doc," Moe said. "I was talkin' to this man. You *are* the one that killed them, aren't you?" he asked Will.

"I'm the one," Will said.

"You see them two fellas standin' over at the bar?" Moe asked.

When Will looked he saw two men, one large and clean-shaven, the other of medium build with a sweeping handlebar mustache. Both were looking toward the table.

"That is Isaac and Amos McAfee. Ernest and Leo worked for them. They're all broke up over losin' a couple of good hands, like they done."

"I could tell, this morning, just how upset you boys must be over Ernest Fowler and Leo Bell getting killed. You showed it at their funeral," Will said. "Oh, wait, that's right, there was no funeral, was there?"

"We're plannin' one," Moe said.

"You're a little late. They buried them this morning," Will said. "They were laid out in plain pine boxes then buried on the far side of Boot Hill without even a marker."

"How do you know?"

"Because I was there," Will answered. "And I was the only one, except for the two grave diggers."

"You always go to the buryin' of men you kill?" Moe asked.

Will flashed a cold look at Moe. "When I can," he answered pointedly. "Sometimes I bury them myself."

Moe didn't expect that answer and he blanched, before he recovered what composure he was able to muster, in his drunken state. "Just how many men have you killed?"

"As many as I needed to."

"Yeah? Well, that don't scare me none."

"Mr. Tucker, you seem to be working yourself into a state," one of the other players said. "Why don't you stop talking about it now, so we can play a friendly game of cards?"

"He's right," Doc Hawkins said. "Quit running your mouth, Tucker. Play cards or get the hell away from my table."

"This ain't your table, Doc. And it sure as hell ain't your fight," Moe said. "It's my fight. Mine and his." He looked, pointedly, at Will.

Slowly, Will unbuckled his pistol belt and hooked it across the back of Doc's chair.

"It isn't anybody's fight," Will said. "Yesterday I was

forced into a situation not of my making, and I wound up killing two men. I don't want to have to kill you too. So, why don't you just calm down? As you can see, I'm not armed."

Moe's features twisted into what might have been a grin. "Well now, taking off your gun like that to keep from fighting might make some folks take you for a coward. You ever thought about that?"

Will looked into Moe's eyes with a glare that was so intense that, for the moment, Moe could forget who was armed and who wasn't.

"You wouldn't be calling me a coward, now, would you, Tucker?" Will asked. His voice was quiet, and his hands were steady, but the look in his eyes was deadly. "Because, I don't think I would like that."

Moe, seeing Will's pistol hanging across the back of Doc's chair, suddenly realized that he had the advantage, and he was emboldened by that fact. He chuckled, derisively. "So, you don't like it? What can you do about it? You ain't even carryin' a gun," he teased.

Will moved so fast then that the others at the table barely saw it. Before Moe knew what was happening, the barrel of his own gun was poking into his nose.

"I don't need to carry a gun as long as fools like you do," Will said easily. "Anytime I want one, I'll just take yours."

Out of the corner of his eye, Will saw Doc draw his

own gun, and for a moment he wondered if Doc was drawing against him. Then he saw Doc pointing his gun toward the bar.

"You two gents take your gun belts off and hand them to the bartender, then get on out of here," Doc said to them. "I intend to keep this altercation between the two of them."

Nodding his thanks, Will turned his attention back to Moe. By now, a tiny trickle of blood was flowing from Moe's nose as a result of the pressure from the gun barrel.

"Now, I'll ask you again. Did you mean to call me a coward?"

"No," Moe stammered. "No, of course not. I was just sayin' that people who won't fight, well, sometimes other people might not understand."

"Is that so?" Will asked. He brought the gun down to his side and one by one, emptied the chambers of Moe's pistol. Then, when it was empty, he handed it back to him.

Moe put his pistol in his holster, then held his handkerchief to his bloody nose. "I've got better things to do than throw my money away," he said. "I could be down to the Carnation House with a woman."

"No, I don't think so," Doc said.

"Why not?"

"Because Miss Lacoste has let it be known that you aren't welcome there."

"Yeah? Well there ain't no town marshal now, so just who the hell is goin' to keep me from goin' if I want to?"

"I will," Doc said simply.

Moe looked at Doc for a moment, then shrugged. "Well, the girls there aren't the only whores in town." Salvaging what bravado he had remaining, Moe turned and walked out of the saloon, followed by Isaac and Amos McAfee.

Shortly after Moe and the McAfees left, Doc Hawkins had another coughing fit and, because this one seemed to go on, he excused himself from the table and walked over to the bar.

"Deal me out of this hand," Will said, taking his money from the table.

A couple of saloon patrons had been waiting for the opportunity to get into the game, and they took the empty chairs as soon as Will and Doc left.

Will stepped up to the bar alongside Doc Hawkins, who was pouring himself a drink. "You all right?" Will asked.

"Yeah, Crockett, I'm fine," Doc replied. He poured Will a drink.

Will was surprised that Doc had called him by name. Neither he nor Gid had given their name since arriving in Shafter yesterday. They were still wanted men in some areas of the country, so as a general rule they didn't advertise who they were.

"Have we met?" Will asked.

"Back when I was bounty hunting, I ran across some dodgers on you and your brother," Doc replied. "The drawings weren't all that good. But you two fit the general description. You'd be Will, I take it?" Doc tossed down his drink

"Yes," Will answered. "You still a bounty hunter?"

"Nope," Doc said. "And if I were, you wouldn't have any worry. As far as I know, you aren't wanted in Texas. The wanted posters I saw were in Dodge City."

"Yeah, they would be in Kansas," Will replied. "I reckon the ones who rode with Quantrill would be wanted in Kansas a hundred years from now, if anyone is still around."

"We all have our crosses to bear," Doc said, taking another drink.

Deep in Doc's eyes Will could see a soul that, for some reason, was badly scarred. Will had seen such eyes during the war. Such men, he knew, were the most dangerous of all, because they didn't care if they lived or died.

"Hey, Doc. Give us a tune, will you?" someone called from the other end of the bar.

"Yeah, play somethin' on the piano."

"You can play the piano?" Will asked.

"A little," Doc replied. Shrugging, he walked over to the old scarred piano and sat down. He began playing "Lorena," and all conversation and laughter stopped during the song.

Chapter Three

It was ten o'clock at night and it was cold in Memphis, Tennessee. Polly Carpenter pulled the lap robe around her and settled back in the seat of the hired cab. On the seat in front of her the driver flicked his whip lightly toward the horse. The horse exhaled clouds of vapor that floated away, white, in the night air.

The horse's hooves clopped hollowly on the cobblestone pavement of First Street as they passed the dark stores and businesses of the commercial district of Memphis. Here and there a yellow square of light shone from the third or fourth floor of the quiet buildings.

Somewhere in the distance a dog began to bark; his bark was answered by another, a little closer. A bottle crashed in a nearby alleyway and a man laughed drunkenly. Polly twisted around to see how close the laughing man was to the hack, and the driver chuckled.

"Don' you be worryin' none, sonny. As long as you in my hack, you under my protection. They ain't nobody goin' to come outta no alley and bother any of my passengers. I can promise you that."

Polly smiled. The driver was a big, strong-looking man and she was fairly certain he could make good his promise of protection. She also smiled at the fact that her disguise was working. He didn't realize she was a woman.

A moment later the hack stopped, and the driver twisted around in his seat.

"Here's the railroad depot," he said. "I don't know where you're goin', but I'd sure like to go with you. Fact is, I'd like to take me a trip 'bout anywhere. I ain't never been nowhere but right here in Memphis."

"Thank you very much," Polly Carpenter said as she paid the driver. Carrying her small bag, she hurried across Poplar Avenue and into the Illinois Central Railroad depot.

Inside the depot a small potbellied stove roared and cracked. The gold light of the fire shone around the cracks and winked through the little vents of the door, and though it put out a small circle of heat immediately around it, it wasn't effectively warming the entire room. Outside it was cold and damp and there was a promise of snow in the air.

Most Memphians would welcome the snow in the

belief that it would wipe out the last vestige of the yellow fever with which the city had suffered for the past five years.

Of course, even if the fever did break it would be too late for Polly. It wouldn't bring her parents back. She would still be left with no known relative except the man her mother had married after her father died. Frank Sweeny had been a foreman in her father's cotton brokerage firm, and Polly's mother married him because she felt inadequate to the task of running the firm alone. Then, six months ago, Polly's mother had also died.

Sweeny had convinced Polly's mother to change her will on her deathbed so that Polly wouldn't come into her inheritance until she was twenty-five or married, whichever occurred first. "In the meantime, I think you should appoint me as her administrator," he told Polly's mother. "That way I can look out for her until she is mature enough to look out for herself."

Recently, Sweeny had been putting pressure on Polly to marry him. That was something she would never do, so taking $200, which was the most cash she could get her hands on, she planned a midnight escape.

Pulling the brim of her hat down and the collar of her coat up, Polly walked over to the ticket window. There were at least a dozen people in the waiting room, and though none of them paid any particular attention to her, she felt as if every eye could see through her disguise. She needn't have worried. The heavy winter clothes did a good job of concealing her true gender.

"Well, lad, and where would you be going this cold night?" the ticket agent asked.

Polly paused. It was funny but not until this moment had she considered where to go. She had only thought of fleeing—she had not thought of where she would go. "Well, I—I don't know," she stammered.

"You have to have something in mind, at least a direction. Which is it? North, south, east, or west?" the ticket agent asked.

"West."

"Where in the West? Texas? California? Arizona Territory?"

"Texas," Polly answered.

The ticket agent chuckled. "I should'a known it. You've been readin' the penny awfuls, haven't you? You're goin' west to be a cowboy."

"Yes, that's it," Polly said. "I want to be a cowboy."

The ticket agent began tearing off tickets and stamping them with a rubber stamp. "Can't say as I blame you. If I was young, I might be doin' that myself. I've been reading about a silver mine out in West Texas. Closest town to it is Shafter. If you're looking for adventure, you might go there."

"All right, I'd like a ticket to Shafter," Polly said without further thought.

"First thing you're going to have to do is go south. You'll leave this train in Jackson, Mississippi, then you'll catch the Southern Pacific. That'll take you all the way to Marfa."

"Marfa? I thought you said Shafter."

"I did, but there's no railroad in Shafter. You'll have to take a stagecoach from Marfa to get to Shafter."

"How long will the trip take?"

"Oh, 'bout a week," the ticket agent said. He took Polly's money and handed her a tag for her baggage. "Just have a seat over there, son. We'll call your train in about half an hour."

"Thank you."

Polly found a seat within the circle of warmth from the stove and had almost dozed off when the windows of the station began to rattle, and the very floors of the stationhouse started to shake. The sound of the train was much louder now, not just the whistle, but the rush of steam and the roar of steel rolling on steel. The darkness outside the depot windows was suddenly bathed in a bright light and when Polly looked outside, she saw that the threatened snow had materialized. The falling snowflakes glistened like diamonds in the beam of the approaching engine's headlamp.

Ten minutes later, with Polly in a seat most distant from any other occupied seat, the train pulled out of the Memphis depot with a series of jerks and clanks. As the train rolled through the dark city, the conductor came through the cars, turning down the gas lamps so that soon it was as dark inside as out. Polly pulled her coat up around her, made herself as comfortable as possible, and settled in for the long trip.

Carnation House

"What did you say?" Marie asked.

"I said, why don't you let me take you out to get something to eat?" Gid repeated.

"You bought me a drink, that's enough." She lifted a glass from the table. "What makes you think you have to wine and dine me?"

"Oh, I don't know, it's just that when I find a pretty woman like you, I like to take her out and show her off."

Marie laughed again. "I'm a madam, Gid. I run a whore house. People don't show off whores."

"I do," Gid said. "Besides, I'm hungry."

"Then, why don't you let me have the cook fix you something? Señor Munoz is a wonderful cook."

"No," he said. "We're goin' out."

"Gid," Marie said, and this time her voice was quiet

and apologetic. "Don't you know how it is with women like me? I don't want to embarrass you, but they won't even let me in the Hermitage. You would understand why, if you knew that half the men in there at any given time are regular customers here."

"You'll be with me," Gid said, resolutely. "They'll let you in."

Marie sat there for a moment longer, then she laughed.

"All right, why the hell not? I'd like to see the expressions on their faces anyway. Besides, if I'm with a big, strong fella like you, who would dare keep me out? So, I'll go with you," Marie said. "But on one condition."

"What's the condition?"

"I want you to leave your gun here."

"Why?"

"Because if you do feel it is necessary to *defend my honor,*" she emphasized the words, teasingly, "I don't want any shooting. You can break a nose if you need to, but I don't want anyone killed."

"All right," Gid said, laying his gun on the table. "If you say so." He chuckled.

"What are you laughing at?"

"Darlin', just so you know, if I wanted to kill someone, I wouldn't really need a gun."

Marie drew hostile stares when they went into the Hermitage Café several minutes later, but because nobody wanted to confront the big man who was with her, no one made any effort to deny her entry. The waiter came up to their table as Gid was holding the chair for Marie to be seated.

"Good evening, Louis, how are you?" Marie asked.

"Please, Miss Marie," Louis said, looking around nervously. "You mustn't let on that you know me."

"All right," Marie said, more quietly. "I don't want to cause you any trouble. What do you recommend, tonight?"

"Tonight, *mademoiselle*, I recommend the Tournedos Hermitage," Louis said, once more affecting his cultured accent. "It is a delightful cut of beef, delicately sautéed and served on a bed of marinated artichoke hearts."

"Excellent," Marie said. "I'll have that."

"I will too," Gid said, taking his own seat now. "But you'd better double my order. Most of the time those foreign sounding dishes don't have enough food on the plate to suit me."

"Very good," Louis said, retiring to see to their order.

A few moments later the front door opened, and a man stepped inside. He was obviously drunk, and he almost lost his balance, but he caught himself on the doorframe. The action caused his hat to fall off and when he picked it up, Gid saw that it was decorated with a band of silver conchos. He knew then that this was no ordinary cowboy.

A working cowboy would not be able to keep such a hat for long; during the frequent lean times, he would surely sell the silver conchos.

"Marie, you in here?" he called from the door. "Marie!" he yelled. He put the hat back on his head.

"Oh, no," Marie said under her breath. She raised the menu in front of her.

"What?" Gid asked. "Who is that?"

"That is Moe Tucker," Marie said. "He's nothing but a troublemaker and I've forbidden him to ever enter the Carnation House.

"So, there you are Marie," Moe said, seeing her for the first time. "I heard you was in here." He started toward her but tripped over a chair. He prevented himself for falling, only by grabbing onto another diner.

"You are drunk, sir!" the diner said indignantly. "You've no business on the streets, bothering innocent people."

"What's that?" Moe asked. He pushed his jacket open and put his hand, menacingly, over his pistol. "You tellin' me what to do?"

"Leave him alone, Moe," Marie said, speaking up then. "What is it? What do you want?"

"I want to come to your whorehouse," Moe said. "I promise to behave myself."

"You're not welcome," Marie said.

"Why ain't I welcome? My brother's always welcome."

"Lenny is a well-behaved young man," Marie said. "You are not. Now, please leave. You are causing a disturbance in here."

"Oh, I'm causing a disturbance, am I? Well, Marie, you ain't seen nothin' yet. Wait 'till you see the disturbance I'm goin' to cause in your whore house if you don't—"

Gid stood up then and took a step toward Moe. Moe stopped. "Who are you?"

"I'm a friend of Miss Lacoste's," Gid said. "Why don't you go away like she said?"

For a moment Moe was intimidated by Gid's size and obvious strength; then he noticed that Gid wasn't wearing his gun. Quickly, he drew his own and he pointed it at Gid.

"You stay right there, you big son of a bitch," Moe said. Gid stopped and Moe smiled. "I ought to gut-shoot you right now, you bastard, for butting into business that's none of your concern," Moe said.

"Tucker!" a new voice called.

Moe recognized Doc Hawkins' voice and the mocking smile left his face to be replaced with one of grim determination. He appeared to have sobered up immediately.

"Doc, you wouldn't shoot me in the back, would you?" Moe asked.

"I never could figure out the concern whether someone was shot in the back or the front," Doc said. "What's the point? You'll be dead either way. Right now, I've got a gun pointed toward the back of your head, and if you so much as twitch, I'm going to shoot you where you stand."

There was no gun pointed toward the back of Moe Tucker's head. In fact, Doc wasn't even wearing a gun.

"I ... I ain't movin'," Moe said nervously.

"Then put your gun back in your holster and get out of here," Doc ordered.

"I'm doin' it, I'm doin' it," Moe said, holstering his pistol. He turned then and started toward Doc. That was when he saw that Doc wasn't armed.

"Why, you son of a bitch, you wasn't pointin' no gun at me!" Moe said. His hand started to dip toward his own pistol, but he never reached it because Gid stepped up to him and laid him out in one punch. Moe went down with his arms flung to either side of him.

"Thanks, for takin' a hand in this, mister," Gid said.

"Call me Doc," Doc said. "Your brother does."

"You know my brother?"

"Will Crockett? Yes. We met over a game of cards. I'm Doc Hawkins."

Like his brother, Gid had heard of Doc Hawkins. And, like Doc Hawkins, many in the restaurant had heard of Gid and Will Crockett. Gid realized then that any anonymity the brothers may have had when they arrived in town was gone now.

Glad to meet you, Doc," Gid said. "Won't you join Miss Lacoste and me for supper?"

"Thanks, but no thanks," Doc said. "I was just walking by when I saw what was going on in here. I'm going to get a bottle of whiskey and have a few drinks before I turn in. And I've never liked to drink on a full stomach," he added cynically. He touched the brim of his hat, then left.

"What are you going to do about him?" Louis asked, pointing to Moe. In his frustration, Louis had lost his carefully nurtured, cultured accent.

"I'll take him outside until he sobers up," Gid said.

Gid picked Moe up and threw him over his shoulder as easily as if he were handling a sack of flour. Moe's hat lay on the floor; Marie picked it up and placed it on Moe's upturned butt.

"Well, now, I've never seen that fancy silver hat of his look better," one of the restaurant patrons said, and the others laughed at the sight. Several of the customers followed Gid through the door, then watched as Gid dropped Moe into the nearest watering trough.

Chapter Four

It was early morning, and though most self-respecting roosters had announced the fact long ago, half a dozen cocks were still trying to stake a claim on the day. The sun had been up for quite a while, but the disc was still hidden by the Cieniga Mountains to the east. The light had already turned from red to white and here and there were signs of the town rising.

A pump creaked as a housewife began pumping water for her morning chores. The first whistle at one of the mines up in the hills called to the miners and somewhere a carpenter had already begun hammering.

Will was awakened by the early-morning sounds, and he poured a basin of water for his shave. He stood by the open window and looked out on the town. He and Gid had been here for nearly a week now, long enough for him to measure the intensity of the disagreement between the people of the town and the ranchers and cowboys of the county.

Under normal circumstances Will believed he would have sided with the cattlemen's position. The cowboys were rugged men who were more at home in the saddle than in a parlor, and Will and Gid related to that.

But the townspeople regarded the Tuckers and the McAfees and the cowboys who worked for them not as rugged individualists, but as a bunch of ruffians ... hell-raisers who had grown wild on the range and were only too anxious to let off steam when they came into town. Often, letting off steam meant shooting their guns, if not at each other in some spontaneous duel, then at any target that might catch their fancy.

Regardless of Will's normal predilection, he had been drawn in on the townspeople's side, first when he killed Bell and Fowler, and then again when he and Moe had a run-in. He also found it easy to side with the town because Doc Hawkins, who had become a good friend, was solidly in the camp of the townspeople. And Gid's friend, Marie Lacoste, took the position that, though there was no absolute right or wrong in the conflict, the town was more right than the cattlemen, especially the Tuckers and the McAfees.

The leading troublemaker of all was Moe Tucker. Will had only seen Moe's brother, Lenny, from a distance. Most spoke well of Lenny, even the townspeople, and since the younger Tucker had done nothing to cross him, Will had no reason not to believe that he was the well-behaved young man everyone made him out to be.

As Will shaved, a couple of freight wagons rolled slowly through the streets, just beginning what would be a day-long journey to Marfa. The shop keepers were very busy sweeping the wooden porches and boardwalks clean, the better to attract potential customers. A cowboy who had just awakened from a drunken night on the street was wetting his head in a watering trough.

There was a knock on his door.

"Will? Will, you 'bout ready for some breakfast?" Gid called.

"Yeah," Will said, reaching for his shirt. "I'll be down in a minute."

Gid was waiting on the front porch of the hotel when Will came down. Gid stretched, then took a deep breath. "Beautiful morning, don't you think, Will?"

"I guess so," Will said.

"I like this town," Gid said. "I could stay here, a while."

"That's what you said about the last town."

"Yeah, well, I think that's because I always like where I am, better than any other place," Gid said seriously.

Will looked at Gid trying to figure out what he'd said, then he laughed. "Whatever you say, Little Brother."

They started toward the Hermitage Café, passing the general store on the way. A Mexican was picking through the fruits and vegetables the store owner had on display on the front porch of his store.

"Good morning, Señor Munoz," Gid called, cheerily.

"Good morning, Señor Crockett," the Mexican replied with a polite tip of his hat.

"Damn, Little Brother, do you know everyone in town already?" Will asked.

"Not everyone," Gid replied. "Just the ones who are important. Señor Munoz cooks for the whores over at the Carnation House."

Will laughed again. "Whores and cooks," he said. "Not everyone, just the ones who are important."

Will was having a second cup of coffee and Gid was having another batch of pancakes when three men approached the table, all wearing suits. None were wearing guns. Will had been here long enough now to recognize all of them. The short, bald-headed man with chin whiskers but no mustache, was J.C. Malone, editor of the Shafter newspaper, *The Bi-Weekly Defender.* Malone was also the mayor of the town. Harry Rutledge, a very rotund man with a round face and glasses that magnified his eyes, was the banker. Rupert Jackson, tall and thin with sunken cheeks, black hair, and dark eyes, owned the hardware store and the funeral parlor.

"Gentlemen, excuse us for disturbing you at your breakfast, but I wonder if we might have a few words with you," Malone said.

"Go right ahead, Mayor," Gid replied. "As long as we don't have to stop eatin'." He carved off a large piece of ham and stuck it in his mouth.

"I was just wondering ... that is, we were wondering, how long you were planning on staying around our town?"

Will took a swallow of his coffee and studied the mayor and his delegation over the rim of his cup.

"Are you telling us you want us to leave?" he asked, calmly.

"No!" the mayor barked. "Heavens, no, nothing like that. I hope you wouldn't think that."

"You asked how long we were planning to stay—what did you expect us to think?"

"It's just that, well, since Marshal Vidal was killed, we've been a town without law. And no town can afford to be without law."

"I don't know about that," Will replied. "I've always figured that if everyone sort of minded their own business, there'd be no need for law."

"Yes, well, that's the problem. Everyone doesn't mind their own business," Malone said. He looked over at

Jackson. "Tell them about your, uh, customer," he said.

"Yes," Jackson replied. "It's a terrible thing. As you gentlemen may know, in addition to owning the hardware store, I am also the town undertaker."

"Yes, I saw you at the cemetery when Bell and Fowler were buried," Will said.

"What about Sheriff Jones? Doesn't his jurisdiction also include Shafter?"

"I assure you, you will find few in this town who are acolytes of Sheriff Pickney Jones," Rutledge answered. "In my opinion, he represents the interests of the county, at the expense of the interests of merchants of the town."

"Get to the point, Harry," Malone said. "Mr. Crockett, I, as the mayor, and these two gentlemen, representing the town council, would like for you to become our town marshal. And we want your brother to act as your deputy."

Surprised by the offer, Will put his coffee cup down and stared pointedly at the three men. "You want *me* to be the marshal?"

"Yes," the mayor said. "Well, both of you, actually."

"Mr. Mayor, before this goes any farther, perhaps you should know who we are," Will suggested.

"I know who you are. Doc told me. You're the Crockett brothers," Malone said.

"And you also know that there's paper out on us? We're wanted men."

"Are you wanted in Texas?"

Will shook his head. "The governor gave us a pardon, but it's only for the state of Texas."

"Then it doesn't matter to us whether you're wanted someplace else or not."

"Not to you, perhaps. But it might matter to some of your people. Especially when they find out about our background."

"I know about your background as well, Mr. Crockett. The two of you rode with Quantrill," Rutledge said. "I'm from Kansas, and I know better than anyone of the evil perpetrated by the men from Missouri. My own brother rode with Jim Lane and was killed during an encounter with the Bushwhackers. If I had seen you—or any of Quantrill's riders—during that time, I would have gladly killed you myself. But the war is over, and times have changed. Now I'm the banker in a town that is in desperate need of a lawman. I tell you true, to protect my business interests here, I would make a bargain with the devil himself if I had to."

Will chuckled. "And you consider us the devil?"

"I do indeed, sir, I do indeed. But I make no bones about it," Rutledge admitted. "This is rough country out here. Perhaps we need the devil on our side."

"Suppose some of those reward posters on us show up?" Gid asked. "Wouldn't it be a little embarrassing to the town council to have law officers who are wanted men?"

"Why should it be?" Jackson asked. "Who would be in better position to destroy any old reward dodgers than someone in the marshal's office?"

Gid chuckled. "Yeah," he said. "He's got a point, Will. We could do that."

"Now, about the pay," the mayor said. "I'm sure you would be interested in knowing how you would be paid."

"Yeah, if I'm going to take a job, I'd like to know how much I'll make," Will said.

"Fifty dollars a month to each of you. The town will pick up the cost of your rooms at the hotel where you are staying now, and the cost of anything you eat here at the Hermitage."

Will laughed. "I take it you haven't seen Gid eat," he said. "But I have to tell you, even with his appetite, I don't know that it's worth it. I've only been here for a week and I already know there's a showdown coming. Fifty dollars a month doesn't seem to me to be enough money to be caught in the middle of it."

"Yes," Rutledge said. He cleared his throat. "That's why we have passed a special gambling tax."

"Gambling tax?"

"From now on, the dealer of every card game in town will withhold ten percent of every pot," Rutledge said. "That ten percent will go to your office."

"Ten percent of every hand will go to us? What would Doc think about that?" Will asked.

"The gambling tax was Doc's idea," Malone answered. "It was also his suggestion that we ask you two to take the marshal job. He visited with me just before he left."

"Doc left?"

"Yes, but only to go to El Paso. He'll be back in a few days. I understand he had some business of some sort," Malone said.

"I wonder what sort of 'business' Doc could have in El Paso?" Jackson mused.

"I don't know," Malone answered. He smiled. "But I sure wouldn't want to be the businessman who is crossing him."

"Tell me, Mayor, just how much money would we make from that gambling tax?" Gid asked.

"Suppose I let Mr. Rutledge answer that," Malone said. "He is the banker, after all."

Rutledge cleared his throat. "I must tell you that, when I figured out just how large your take would be, I was opposed to it. My suggestion was that the money should come directly to the town, and the town could then draw from it to pay you a somewhat better salary. But the council overrode my suggestion, opting to give all the money directly to you."

"How much?" Will asked, repeating his brother's

question.

"In my estimation, a minimum of one thousand dollars per month," Rutledge said.

Will whistled. "And that's not against the law?" he asked.

"The town council voted for it," Malone said. "That makes it legal."

"One thousand dollars a month!" Gid said. "Damn, Will, I didn't know it was possible to make that much money, legally. Who wants to try our hand at mining silver?"

"I agree, we're out of the mining business. Mr. Mayor, you have yourself a couple of marshals," Will said as he extended his hand.

"Good," Malone replied. "Now, when can you start?"

"We've already started," Will replied.

Roscoe Gentry sat at the desk in the sheriff's office. Jones told him it wasn't necessary for him to stay on duty tonight, but Gentry liked to be in the office at night. It helped him to think.

Gentry poured himself a cup of coffee, then laced the cup liberally with whiskey. He stepped over to the window and looked down the long street toward the downtown part of Shafter.

He'd learned today that Shafter had hired new law. Will and Gid Crockett, the two men who had only recently arrived in town, were now the town marshal and deputy marshal.

Will was good, too. Gentry had seen him in action. Not so much the way he killed Leo Bell. After all, he and Bell were both holding a gun on each other and Crockett was the only one smart enough to pull the trigger. Gentry took a drink of his whiskey-laced coffee. Hell, he thought, anyone should have enough sense not to just stand there and let the other fella shoot ... not when you were holding a gun on each other.

No, it was the other thing, the way Will had drawn his gun and fired—almost in the same action—at Ernest Fowler. Fowler was standing at the top of the stairs, holding a shotgun, but he was still killed. Gentry was impressed by that.

He took another swallow of his drink, then walked back over to refill his cup.

El Paso

Doc Hawkins was sitting in a straight-backed wooden chair in a doctor's office located on the second floor over a furniture store. The diploma on the wall indicated that Jason Harby, M.D., had graduated from the Ohio School of Medicine in Cincinnati, Ohio. There were other totems of his profession scattered about the office as well: a tall glassed-in apothecary case, an examining table, charts on the wall depicting the human anatomy, and a well-worn leather medicine bag.

Doc Hawkins, who had come to El Paso specifically to see Dr. Harby, had another coughing fit. He held his handkerchief over his mouth until the seizure passed, then put the handkerchief away and looked at Dr. Harby.

"How often do these coughing seizures come?" Dr. Harby asked.

"The really bad ones come at a rate of about one an hour," Doc answered. "The easier ones come more often."

"Do you suffer from the runs? And vomiting?"

"Yes."

"Sweating at night?"

"Yes."

"How long since you started coughing up sputum?"

"I've been doing it for about six months," Doc answered. "I kept waiting for it to go away but it never did. The blood has only been about a month."

"And the vomiting and the runs?"

"About a month."

"I know you are called Doc Hawkins. Is that just what they call you? Or, are you really a doctor? The reason I ask is, I want to know how best to describe your condition to you."

"I am a doctor," he said. "But not a medical doctor. I am a PhD."

"A PhD?" Dr. Harby asked in surprise.

Doc laughed. "It's sort of funny, isn't it? A wasted degree. But then, mine has been a wasted life. However, I believe I will be able to comprehend whatever you have to tell me."

"I'm sure you've guessed it by now. You are suffering from pulmonary phthisis. It is more commonly known as consumption. Some doctors refer to it as tuberculosis because of the tubercles, or fine granules which are found in the lungs."

"Is there anything that can be done for it?" Doc asked. "Anything I can take? I've seen ads in newspapers."

Dr. Harby shook his head. "Quackery, all of it," he replied. "If I had my way, anyone who advertised their snake oil to cure what can't be cured would be horsewhipped and thrown in jail."

"So, there is nothing to be done?"

"Well, there are places where you can go," Dr. Harby said. "Consumption asylums. If you go to one and do what they tell you to do, you can prolong your life."

"Prolong it for how long?"

"You have what is called fibrocaseous tuberculosis. Fortunately, it is the slowest acting form of the disease. With supervised care in an asylum, you could live for another five years."

"And if I chose not to go to an asylum?"

"A year, if you do nothing for yourself, maybe three years if you are careful."

"Thanks," Doc said.

"I could get you a list of asylums."

"No, thanks. I'll take care of myself. I'd rather live three years free ... hell, I'd rather live one year free, than five in a jail."

"They aren't jails," Dr. Harby said. "Some of them are really quite comfortable."

"No, thank you, no asylum for me. All right, what should I do for myself?"

"Get as much fresh air as you can. Always sleep with a window open, but sleep under a blanket, and wear warm clothing. And of course, no more smoking and no more drinking. That is very important. Also, drink as much milk as you can, eat as much meat as you can."

"I have no appetite for food," Doc said.

"Yes, I know, that is one of the really insidious things about this disease. The very thing that you must do in order to survive is difficult because of the lack of appetite brought on by the illness."

"And if I do all these things you tell me, can you guarantee that it will give me three more years?"

"It may. Of course, there is always the possibility that

it won't help at all."

"So, what you are saying is, I have from one to three years, no matter what I do?"

"If you do nothing to take care of yourself, you won't last over a year. That, I *can* guarantee you."

Doc was quiet for a moment, then he reached for his jacket.

"All right," he finally said. "Thank you, Doctor."

"Doctor Hawkins," Harby said as Doc was putting on his jacket. Doc looked at him.

"I have heard of you. I know who you are, and the type of life that you lead. And I know that nothing I have told you today is going to change anything. But I had to tell you."

"I understand."

"There is one more thing that I think you should understand. One of the cruelest aspects of this disease is how infectious it is. You can quite easily give it to the ones you care for the most. Women, for example. If you are ever with a woman ... even for something as innocent as a kiss, there is a very good chance that you will infect her."

Doc was silent for a moment, then, almost imperceptibly, he nodded.

"I understand," he said.

Chapter Five

It was hot when Polly arrived in Marfa, Texas. It had been less than a week since she left the snowy cold of Memphis, such a sharp contrast in so short a time seemed unreal. She took her jacket off and tossed it across her shoulder, then braced herself to walk from the shade provided by the roofed platform into the bright Texas sun.

An old Mexican woman was operating some sort of food stand right across the street from the railroad depot. The old woman didn't have any teeth and she kept her mouth closed so that her chin and nose nearly touched. A swarm of flies buzzed around the steaming kettles, drawn by the pungent aromas of meat and sauces. She worked with quick, deft fingers, rolling the spicy ingredients into something that looked like pie crust, then wrapping them in old newspapers before she handed them to her customers.

Polly was curious about the food, so she walked over to the old woman.

"What is this you are selling?" she asked.

"Tacos," the old woman said. "Very good. You try."

"How much?"

"Five cents."

Polly took out a nickel and handed it to the old woman, who quickly put together a taco and handed it back to her.

"Hey, tenderfoot, those things go down a lot better with a beer," someone called. "Or, don't you have beer back east?"

"Yes, we most assuredly do have beer," Polly said.

"Yes," *the man mimicked*. "We most assuredly do have beer."

Polly was surprised by the bantering tone of the man. She had done nothing to antagonize him. Why was he so belligerent? She glanced over toward the man who was tormenting her and flashed him a look of irritation.

The man was leaning against the front of an adobe building with his arms folded across his chest and one leg bent at the knee so that his foot was against the wall. He appeared to be in his twenties, with a dark handlebar mustache and a cowlick of the same color across his forehead. He was dressed in a red checkered shirt and denim trousers with leather chaps. There were two other men similarly dressed who were standing near him, though they hadn't spoken. They were all wearing guns. This was the first time that Polly had ever seen anyone other than a police officer, wearing a gun.

"I don't like that look on your face, tenderfoot. What are you a'lookin' at?" the man asked, standing up straight and letting his arms fall down loosely to his side.

"Apparently I am looking at an ill-mannered boor," Polly said. She looked away from him then, satisfied that she had put him in his place and hoping that if she dropped it right here, he would go away and leave her alone.

"What'd you call me, boy?" the man blustered. "A boar? Ain't that a hog? You callin' me a dirty pig?"

"No," Polly said. "That's not what I said."

"The hell it ain't. You insulted me, mister. You called me a pig."

"Please," Polly said, growing a little frightened now. This was getting out of hand. "I don't want any trouble."

"Well, you already got trouble, mister, and plenty of it," the man said. "Nobody calls me a pig and gets away with it."

"Please, I'm sorry if I insulted you," Polly said. She was getting a little frightened now. What had she done? How had she gotten into such a situation? All she did was buy something to eat.

"You packin' a gun, tenderfoot?"

"What? No, no, of course not," Polly answered nervously. "Why would I want to carry a gun?"

"If you are goin' to go 'roun' callin' folks a pig, you'd best start packin' a gun to back you up. Some folks might not be as nice as I am. I'm goin' to give you a chance to defend yourself. Claude, give 'im your gun. I'm goin' to shoot the son of a bitch, but I want it to be fair 'n square."

"What?" Polly asked, gasping for breath. She dropped her taco and put her hand up to her throat. "What are you saying?"

"I'm sayin', mister', that I'm goin' to gut-shoot you right here 'n leave you for crow bait. But I aim to give you a chance. Give 'im your gun, Claude."

"Buster, this here boy is just a kid. Leave him alone. Hell, he don't even look like he's shavin' yet. Look at that fuzzy cheek."

"Either give the tenderfoot your gun or use it yourself," Buster said menacingly. "It don't make no never-mind to me. I'd just as soon shoot one of you as the other." He turned to face the man who, a moment earlier, had been his friend. He moved his hand to let it hover just over the handle of his revolver.

Polly couldn't believe what was happening. This fool was bent on killing someone and it didn't seem to make any difference to him who it was. He was ready to shoot his own friend if necessary.

"No, no," Claude said in a frightened voice. He began unbuckling his pistol belt. "I'll give 'im my gun."

"Son, do you really want to fight this pig? Or would you allow me the pleasure of killing him?" a new voice asked. The voice was low and resonant, and the words, though as dramatic as any words Polly had ever heard, were spoken in such an offhand way that one might think he was passing an innocent remark about the weather.

Polly looked at this new player upon the stage. He was tall and thin, with black hair and black eyes, and, except for a maroon brocaded vest, dressed in black from his wide-brimmed hat to his boots. He was casually lighting a long, thin cheroot, but Polly noticed that he, like the other men, also wore a gun. The bottom of his jacket was pushed behind the gun to allow him an unrestricted access.

"On second thought," the man went on just as easily, "calling this son of a bitch a pig does a disservice to all the pigs of the world."

Claude stopped unbuckling his gun belt and he and the other man moved quickly out of the way. Even the old taco woman moved back. Only Polly, who was new to this country and inexperienced in assessing the raw passions which governed its inhabitants, remained in harm's way.

Buster turned purple with anger, but something inside checked it. Anyone who could so coldly and deliberately utter killing words had to be someone to be reckoned with.

"Mister, I got no quarrel with you," Buster finally said. "My quarrel is with this here, fella."

"Seems to me like you just sort of picked a quarrel with him," the man in black said.

"He called me a pig."

"Is that a fact? In that case, I think you should thank him for elevating your status."

"What makes you think I'd want to do a fool thing like that?"

"Because I'll kill you if you don't."

Buster laughed nervously. "You'll kill me? And who the hell are you?"

"John is my Christian name," the man said. "But most folks just call me Doc."

"Doc? What are you? A doctor?" Buster laughed. "A doctor is calling down Buster Cox?"

"Yes. Doc Hawkins."

The expression on Buster's face froze. What had been mere nervousness suddenly gave way to pure panic. Beads of perspiration popped out on his upper lip. "Doc Hawkins? You're Doc Hawkins?"

"At your service," Doc said. He flicked an ash from the end of his cheroot.

"I don't believe it. Anyone could step up 'n call themselves Doc Hawkins. That don't mean they are."

"You do have a point there. It could be that I'm not Doc Hawkins, that I'm just telling you that."

"So, you're sayin' you ain't Doc Hawkins?"

"Oh, no, my good man, you're the one saying that I'm not. Of course, you can always put your theory to test by drawing your gun against me."

There was something in the casual way the man in black challenged him that made Buster know, without doubt, that Doc Hawkins was exactly who he said he was.

Buster put both his hands up in the air then backed away. "I ... look, Doc," he stuttered. "I was just havin' a little fun, here. I wasn't really goin' to shoot 'im or anything."

"Tell the boy thank you for calling you a pig," Doc said.

Buster looked at Polly. "What?" he gasped.

"You heard me. Thank the boy for calling you a pig."

"I ... I want to thank you for callin' me a pig," he stammered.

"Do you think he's sincere, boy? Or should I just shoot the son of a bitch now?" Doc asked Polly.

"No!" Polly said. "No, I'm convinced he is quite sincere. Really, I am."

"All right," Doc said easily. He nodded his head slightly. "You and your friends get out of here, and if I hear of this boy so much as stubbing his toe, I'm coming after you."

"Don't worry, Doc, we aren't going to do anything, I

swear," Buster said, and he took one or two hesitant steps, then he and his two comrades broke into a run.

Despite the close call, or perhaps in relief from its passing, Polly laughed at the sight, and she was joined in laughter by the old taco woman.

"Here," the old woman said, making another taco. "You drop one before."

"Thanks," Polly said. She started to pay again but the old woman just waved her hand.

"No pay," she said.

Polly turned to her benefactor.

"I want to thank you too," she said. "I really didn't call him a pig, you know."

"Yeah," Doc said. "Well, I just wish you fellas would wait until you're dry behind the ears before you come out here."

Doc turned and walked away then, as easily as if he had done no more than provide directions.

Polly wondered about the kind of place she had come to. She had been frightened to death, and yet despite the fear she knew she had never been more alive than at the moment of her greatest peril.

Polly checked into a hotel, signing the register only as P. Carpenter.

"That'll be a quarter a night," the clerk said. "Payable

in advance."

Polly gave the clerk a dollar bill and the clerk took a key from a nail. "You're in room three-twelve. That's the top floor, last room to the rear."

"Thank you," Polly said. "Oh, does that have a bath?"

"I can have a tub and some water brought up," the clerk said.

"Please do," Polly said.

Five minutes later a young Mexican boy arrived at her room carrying a tub on his back. He then made several trips back up, bringing buckets of hot water each time until the tub was filled and steaming. Polly tipped him, then contemplated, with great joy, the bath she was about to have. For almost a week she had bumped along on trains, not relaxing in the luxurious Pullman accommodations, but growing dirtier and more tired in what was called "immigrant class." Never mind that she had lost her identity as a woman during the journey, she had almost been dehumanized. But the thought of a hot bath, clean clothes, a good night's sleep in a real bed, and her rebirth as a woman made all that fall away.

The audience stood in tribute as their thunderous applause filled the auditorium.

"*Monsieur*, you have captivated us all with your brilliant playing. You are the sensation of the year. Tomorrow we leave for Vienna, then—"

"I'm afraid there will be no Vienna. Tomorrow I leave for the United States."

"The United States? But I don't understand. The world is your oyster, *Monsieur*. Why would you go back to the United States? They are fighting a war there."

"That is why I must go. My father has called me back. My homeland, the South, is under siege by invaders from the North. I have an obligation."

"But no ... you are beyond petty squabbles now. You are a man of the world, a true cosmopolitan. What care you of a war between bickering neighbors? I beg of you, *monsieur*, do not return. Your music is a gift from God. You speak of obligation and I agree, you do have an obligation. You have a sacred obligation to share your music with the world."

"I'm sorry, *Monsieur* Guerdon. I must go back."

Doc woke up then, and the feelings of the dream were so vivid that he could almost believe Monsieur Guerdon was there in the room with him. It took a moment for him to realize that he was not in Paris, but in his room over a saloon in Marfa.

Doc got out of bed and walked over to the chiffonier, where he poured water from the porcelain pitcher into a basin. Then he erupted into a fit of coughing that left him weak and gasping for breath. When at last the coughing subsided, he poured himself a glass of whiskey, drank it, then washed his face, lathered it, and began to shave.

Why did he dream of Paris? That had been many years ago ... another lifetime ago, when his name had been on the lips of cultured people throughout Europe, when newspapers had lavished praise on him.

"Is this really all you want out of life?" his father had asked him that morning so long ago. "To be a piano player?"

"Papa, the downstairs dandy in a bawdy house is a piano player. I intend to be a concert pianist."

"And that's what you want?"

They were standing on a pillared porch in front of the great columned mansion that was River Birch Plantation. His father was giving him a going-away picnic, and neighbors and relatives crowded together on the well-kept lawn. Dozens of house slaves hustled about serving food and drink to the guests.

"Yes, Papa, it is."

"But to do nothing with your life but make music, whether in a bawdy house or on a concert stage ... seems like such a waste," his father complained.

"Is it a waste to want to do something to make the world a little more beautiful? When you went to Richmond, last year, didn't you bring back two new paintings?"

"Yes, but that's different."

"Why is it different? You bought the paintings because they are a part of the life you have made for us, Papa. I believe man was meant for more than mere survival, and you have raised me to believe that. Thanks to you, I've been surrounded by elegance and beautiful things."

"It isn't entirely thanks to me. You owe a big thanks to cotton and to the money River Birch Plantation makes."

"Well, then, consider River Birch. This house is as beautiful as a Greek temple. Why do we live in such a mansion when a simple log cabin would protect us from the elements?"

"There's more to a home than a place to get out of the rain. There's—"

"Beauty?"

"Beauty, yes." His father paused for a long moment. "All right, John, I see what you mean."

"Papa, I want to give some beauty back to the world and I know I can do it with my music. I've gone as far as I can go with the teachers in this country. Franz Liszt is the finest teacher in the world, and he has accepted me. I can't pass up an opportunity to study under him."

His father smiled. "All right, go to Europe. You'll get no further argument from me. Besides, I must confess that I remember my own tour of Europe with great fondness. I wasn't married to your mother then, of course, and the women of Paris ... Oh, how beautiful they are! And you shall have your pick." He held up his glass. "You are right, why should I keep you from that? If a concert pianist is what you want to be, son, then I want you to be the best."

John Hawkins did go to Europe to follow his dream. And after he completed his studies with Liszt, the master introduced his star pupil to the European concert stages. But when his honor called him back to defend the South, the thunder of the audiences' applause turned into the crash of artillery. The man who had returned from Europe seeing the world for its beauty learned of its ugliness.

At the war's end, he found there was no home to return to. River Birch was no more, having been sold for taxes. His mother had died, and his father died soon after.

John Hawkins began an American concert tour, but the war had not left him, and he had a hard time differentiating the cheers of adulation from his audiences from the cries of dying men he had heard during the war.

The concert tour became meaningless to him and John Hawkins, Doctor of Music, became "Doc" Hawkins—drifter and gambler. Long, dexterous fingers that were so adept at playing the piano were also good at manipulating cards. And when sore losers challenged his veracity, those same quick hands and nimble fingers proved to be exceptionally good at drawing and shooting a pistol.

Once, John Hawkins' name was on the lips of cultured people everywhere. Now the name Doc Hawkins was on the tongues of the society's refuse. Mothers used his name to frighten children into obedience, and young gunsels dreamed of the fame they would win for themselves if only they could outdraw and kill the man called Doc Hawkins.

Chapter Six

When Polly left her room the next morning there was no question of mistaking her sex. As she went downstairs to take her breakfast in the hotel dining room, she was wearing her best dress and her hair was clean and perfectly set. She was aware of the appreciative glances of the men who were present and, though she had hidden her sex during the train ride out, she welcomed the attention now as proof of having made the full transition back to womanhood. She was also excited about what lay ahead, for this was, she told herself, the first day of the rest of her life.

In school, Polly had been particularly good at mathematics. She had gone on to study bookkeeping under the tutelage of the bookkeeper at the cotton brokerage, mastering the art.

She had initially planned to go on to Shafter, but what

if she could get a job here in Marfa? Wouldn't this be just as good a place to start her new life as Shafter?

After breakfast she would start looking for employment and hoped to use her acquired skills to find a position in a bank or an accounting firm.

Shafter

That evening Will and Gid Crockett attended the showing at the Catbird Theater. They were there because the owners of the theater had gone to great expense to bring in a traveling show, and they needed some assurance that the rowdy crowds would not break up the show.

The Catbird Theater was so named because of the twelve tiny balcony boxes, called "catbird seats," that surrounded the mezzanine. Inside the boxes, those who paid extra for the privilege could either watch the show or close the curtains and visit with the soiled doves who practiced their avocation there.

Will had put a sign at the door informing all patrons to check their firearms before entering the theater. Before the prohibition imposed by Marshal Crockett, there had been gunplay at the Catbird just about every night. Over a hundred bullet holes decorated the curtains and screens around the stage and perforated the huge seminude portrait of "Fatima, the belly dancer."

Will stood leaning against a post at the rear of the theater, looking out over the boisterous crowd. He didn't mind coming here to keep order. The theater owner was willing to pay Will and Gid $100 each for their time, plus they got to see a show.

Gid had taken a walk around inside the theater and was just now returning.

"How are things looking, Little Brother?" Will asked under his breath. He smiled and tipped his hat to one of the girls he recognized from the Carnation House. She was hanging onto the arm of a visiting drummer.

"There are some cowboys over there from the Tucker ranch," Gid said. "They're passing a bottle around and talking brave."

"Are they heeled?" Will asked.

"I think they are," Gid said. "None of them are wearing holsters, but I do believe a couple of them have pistols stuck down in their waistbands."

"What do you say we just mosey over there and stand near 'em?" Will suggested. "That way if they start anything, we'll be ready for them."

"All right," Gid agreed.

Suddenly the band played a fanfare, and, amid shouts, hoots and whistles, the theater owner walked out onto the stage. He stood in front of the closed curtains and held his hands up, asking for quiet.

"Ladies and gents," he called.

"There ain't no ladies present!" someone from the audience yelled, and his shout was greeted with guffaws of laughter.

"Oh yeah? Well, what do you call me, you slack-jawed, weasel-faced son of a bitch?" a painted woman from one of the catbird seats shouted down.

There was more laughter, but the theater owner finally managed to get them quiet again.

"Lovers of the theater," he said. "Tonight, we have an especially thrilling show for you."

The audience applauded and whistled.

"We begin our show with the loveliest burlesque girls to be found anywhere west of the Mississippi. Here they are, the Visions of Art!"

Amid a great deal of whistling and stamping of feet, six beautiful and scantily clad young women began the show. After the girls performed, there was a comedy act between a mustachioed lecherous old man, and a beautiful, innocent young girl.

LECHEROUS OLD MAN: My dear, may I tell you, that you are as lovely as a daisy kissed by the dew?

YOUNG GIRL: Why, it wasn't anybody by that name who kissed me. It was Steve Jones, and I told him I feared everyone would find out.

There were a few other jokes like that one, and then a man billed as "The World's Greatest Magician" made his appearance. He introduced his assistant, a lovely young woman who looked suspiciously like one of the Visions of Art.

"And now, friends, I shall perform a feat the likes of which you have never seen before. My lovely assistant will fire this pistol at me, and I will catch the bullets with my teeth!"

Will had seen the trick before and he knew how it worked. The magician's assistant fired blanks while the magician jerked his head back in a bit of ham acting, then spit out slugs he held concealed in his mouth.

Suddenly, one of the three cowboys from Tucker's Ranch stood up and pointed a revolver toward the stage.

"Catch this one, professor!" he shouted.

Quickly, Gid managed to reach him just in time to deflect his shot, while the terrified magician and his assistant hurried from the stage to the guffaws of the audience. One blow from Gid's big fist knocked the cowboy out, and Gid turned to the others and held out his hand.

"If any of you gents are carrying a gun, you'd better

give them to me now."

The two remaining cowboys looked at each other for a moment; then, with a hangdog look on their faces, they pulled pistols from their waistbands and handed them over.

Gid picked up the one he had knocked out and tossed him over his shoulder.

"I'll let him spend the night in jail," he said. "Maybe his manners will be better in the morning, when he's sober."

Gid was back to the theater in time to see the concluding acts. Then, after the curtain came down, most of the audience started down the street for the Dust Cutter Saloon. Will and Gid stood at the door and watched the theater patrons file out, thankful that the three cowboys from Tucker's Ranch had caused them no trouble.

One of the patrons who had enjoyed the show was Dan Rankin. When he came out of the theater, he had a few drinks over at the Dust Cutter with one of the crib whores and thought about availing himself of her services but decided not to. He and his men had been rounding up unbranded calves for the last two days and tomorrow they were going to brand them and turn them out into the herd. It promised to be a busy day, so reason told him he would be better served by returning to the ranch and going to bed.

The ride back to his ranch took about forty-five minutes, and as soon as he dismounted and started to unsaddle his horse, someone came toward him, moving out of the shadows. It was so dark that Dan couldn't see the person's face and for a moment he thought the worst. Cautiously, he let his hand slip down to rest on his pistol. Then he recognized his foreman by the physical feature that gave him his nickname, and he relaxed.

"Hello, Slim. I thought you would be in bed by now. You and the other boys left at least an hour before I did," Dan said as he returned to the job of unsaddling his horse.

"We got a problem, boss."

"What kind of problem?"

"When we got back home, I went out to Big Horse Canyon to check on the calves we cut out for branding, just to make sure they were all right."

"And?"

"They're gone, boss. Ever' damn one of 'em."

"Damn. How did they get away? Did the fence fall?"

"They didn't get away. Someone took them."

"Rustled?"

"That's what they was, all right," Slim said. "And I know who done it."

"Who?"

Slim had something in his hand, and he held it out to show it to Dan.

"What's that?" Dan asked. "It's too dark to see."

"It's a silver concho," Slim said. "Off someone's hat. I found it out there where we were keeping the cattle."

"There's only one person around here who wears silver conchos on his hat," Dan said.

"Moe Tucker," Slim said, before Dan could.

"Yes."

"I've got all the men up and dressed," Slim said.

"What for?"

"So we can go after the son of a bitch. Don't forget boss, those calves belonged to us, too."

Dan put his hand on Slim's shoulder. "Slim, suppose we did go after him. What would we do but start a range war? Remember, we aren't dealing with your average rustler here. We're dealing with another rancher, and a big one at that. If we go over there with a bunch of men, we aren't going to do anything but get a bunch of men killed."

"So, does that mean we don't do anything at all?"

"We can go see Sheriff Jones," Dan suggested.

"Shit," Slim said, spitting. "What the hell good would that do? Moe Tucker has Sheriff Jones's pecker in his pocket, you know that. And his deputy, Gentry, is such a slimy son of a bitch that I don't see how even Jones can put up with him."

"That may be so," Dan said. "But like it or not, Jones is our only choice right now."

It was hot the next morning as Moe Tucker took a drink of water from his canteen and watched the cattle being herded into the McAfee holding pen for branding. He laughed as he thought of how easy it had been to take them. They were all penned up just waiting to be taken.

Last night, just as Moe had figured, Dan and most of his men were in town watching the show. That had made it very easy for them. Lenny had also gone in to see the show, and that was important because Lenny would not have stood by quietly while Moe, Isaac and Fred took Dan's calves. That was why they were brought here, to the Bar M Bar Ranch, instead of being taken over to the Double T Ranch.

Isaac rode over then and reached for Moe's canteen. He took a drink then used the back of his hand to wipe away the water that dribbled down his chin.

"Hell, this is as easy as takin' candy from a baby. They ain't a brand on a one of 'em," Isaac McAfee said. He laughed. "We'll have 'em all branded in no time. Then Rankin or anyone else will play bloody hell proving these cows didn't belong to us all along."

"How many did we get?" Moe asked.

"Near as I can make out, about a hundred and ten or so," Isaac answered. "And even immature calves is bringin' twelve dollars a head at Marfa, 'n twenty dollars a head at Kansas City. There's several hundred dollars, just slick as a whistle.

Moe laughed. "And Lenny thinks he's the smart one in the family."

Isaac took a chew from a plug of tobacco, then offered the plug over to Moe. "You gonna tell your brother?"

"Hell no, I ain't goin' to tell him," Moe answered. "He's so lily-livered, he'd be for givin' the cows back." Moe took a chew from the proffered plug then handed it back.

"I don't know, Moe," Isaac said. "Sometimes I think you cut your brother a little short. I think if it ever come down to it, he'd take a stand for you."

"If it ever come down to somethin' like that he wouldn't even be around," Moe growled. "You ever seen the little bastard drunk?"

"No."

"No, and you ain't a'gonna, either. I tell you, he's just different from the rest of us, that's all."

"Then if your brother ain't goin' to be in on this, we're goin' thirds, not halves," Isaac said.

"Thirds? What do you mean?"

"I mean a third for Amos, a third for me, and a third for you. Not half for you, and half for me and Amos. Besides, we're the ones runnin' the risk. We're keepin' the cows here until we sell them."

"Won't be no risk once we get your brand on them," Moe said.

Isaac smiled. "That's another thing," he said. "Once we get the McAfee brand on them, if we wanted to, we could claim 'em all an' there wouldn't be nothin' you could do about it. When you look at it like that, we're bein' generous to cut you in for a third."

Moe glared at Isaac, then took his hat off and turned it in his hand for a moment while he thought about what Isaac had said. He ran his hand along the band of conchos and noticed that one was missing. He wondered where it might be.

"What do you say, Moe? Is it a deal?"

Moe sighed, then put his hat back on. "I guess a third is better than nothin'," he said. "I don't reckon I've got any other choice."

Isaac smiled victoriously. "I don't reckon you do," he said. "Come on, we've got some branding to do."

Chapter Seven

"You sure you want to go through with this?" Sheriff Jones asked as he and Dan rode up the long road from the entry gate to the Tucker house. "I mean in these parts callin' a man a cattle rustler is 'bout the worst thing you can say about him."

"I haven't called him a cattle rustler yet," Dan said. "Right now, I'm just wantin' to see if he might have lost a silver concho. You might even say I'm doing him a favor. And, in return for that favor, I'd like to take a ride through some of his stock. Particularly the branding calves, see if perhaps I can find any of mine."

"I thought you said you hadn't branded them yet."

"I hadn't."

"Then how do you plan to recognize them?" Jones asked.

"There's one or two I might recognize," Dan replied.

They reached the front of the house, then got down from their horses and walked up the steps of the front porch. Moe Tucker met them at the door. He greeted Jones, then saw Dan.

"What are you doing here, Rankin?" he asked.

"Mr. Tucker, if you don't mind, I'd like to take a look at some of your calves."

"My calves? What for? You plannin' on buyin' some?"

"He ain't talkin' buyin, Moe," Jones said. "He says some of his cows were stolen."

Moe Tucker glared at Dan for a long moment. "Accusin' us of stealin' ain't very neighborly."

"I'm not accusin' you, Mr. Tucker."

"Then what are you doin' here?"

"Like I said, I'd like to take a look at your brandin' calves."

A horse came around the corner of the house then, and Dan looked over to see Lenny.

"Hi, Dan," Lenny greeted in a friendly voice. He dismounted and started toward him.

"Lenny, this here fella has accused us of cattle rustlin'," Moe said.

Lenny's eyes flinched, and for just a moment Dan saw something like sadness in them. The look passed quickly, however, and Lenny resumed an expression of unruffled calm.

"You know, Rankin," he said quietly, using Dan's last name this time. "There have been folks shot for calling other folks horse and cow thieves."

"I know," Dan replied. "And there have been people hanged for stealing horses and cows."

"Seems to me like we're at an impasse here," Lenny said. "If you're wrong, I ought to shoot you. If you're right, you ought to hang me."

"So far I haven't accused anyone," Dan said. "Like I told your brother, all I want to do is have a look at your brandin' calves."

"All right," Lenny said. "Come on, I'll show you around."

"We ain't got to do that, Lenny," Moe said. He looked at the sheriff. "Unless you got a warrant," he added. "You got one of them things, Jones?"

"No."

"Then you got no business messin' around in our business," Moe said.

"Let me show him around, Moe," Lenny said. "We don't have anything to hide."

Moe was silent for a moment; then he held his arm out, as if in invitation. "Go ahead, Rankin," he said. "Take a look around."

Dan, Lenny, and Sheriff Jones remounted, then rode around the corner of the house out toward the branding pens. There, a hundred or more calves milled about.

"There they are," Lenny said when they reached the pens. Dan dismounted, then climbed up on the fence and started looking out over the calves. Though most calves looked alike, he could remember having noticed three or four with rather distinctive markings during the roundup and he was certain he would be able to recognize them if he saw them now. He stood there for a long moment, staring intently at the small herd.

He saw none that he could identify.

"See any of yours?" Lenny asked.

Dan shook his head. "None I could identify," he admitted. He climbed down from the fence.

"When were these cows supposed to have been stolen?" Lenny asked.

"We finished rounding them up yesterday," Dan said. "We were going to get to the branding today, but my foreman discovered them missing last night."

"What makes you think we took them?" Lenny asked.

Dan looked at Lenny. "The truth is, Lenny, I wouldn't have believed you had anything to do with it, even if I had found them here," he said. "I figure it was that no-good brother of yours."

Lenny squinted his eyes. "Careful, Rankin. Like you said ... he *is* my brother. You got any particular reason for accusin' him?"

Dan pulled the concho from his shirt pocket and showed it to Lenny. "We found this out where the cattle were," he said.

At that moment Moe came up to join them. "Found any of your cows, Rankin?" he asked mockingly.

"No."

"What made you think they would be here?"

"Because he found this where he had been keeping his branding calves," Lenny said, holding out the concho Dan had given him. "The calves are gone."

Moe got down from his horse and went over to take the concho from Lenny. He held it up to his hat, laying it over the place where one was obviously missing. "Well, I'll be damned," he said. "So, that's where it was."

"You got any idea on how it wound up on the ground of my empty cattle pen?" Dan asked.

"Don't have any idea at all," Moe replied. "I prob'ly lost it in town sometime last week."

"You expect me to believe that?" Dan asked.

Moe stared at Dan as he put the hat back on with the concho now in place.

"Yeah," he said. "I expect you to believe it."

"Lenny?" Dan said. "Lenny, I know you aren't a thief. What do you think about this?"

Lenny looked at his brother and, once again, Dan thought he saw a flash of sadness in his eyes.

"I believe my brother, Rankin," Lenny said.

"Come along, Rankin," Sheriff Jones said. "There's nothing more for you out here."

"You *are* going to investigate, aren't you?" Dan asked.

Jones sighed. "Suppose you tell me just what I'm supposed to investigate. You came out here to look at the calves like you wanted. Did you find anything?"

"No."

"Then we're leavin'." The sheriff, who had not dismounted, turned his horse and started to ride away. Frustrated, Dan stood his ground a moment longer. Then, suddenly, he felt something hard poking him in the back. When he turned around, he saw that Moe had pulled his rifle from his saddle scabbard and was pointing it at him.

"Well, if you ain't a'gonna go like the sheriff said, I might just shoot you where you stand," Moe said ominously.

Dan reached his hand out as fast as the strike of a snake and grabbed the rifle away from Moe as clean as a whistle. Moe let out a bellow of surprise and started for his pistol, but Dan brought the butt of the rifle up in a vertical stroke, catching Moe under the chin. Moe went down and Dan whirled and had the rifle leveled toward Lenny in almost the same moment, catching Lenny with the pistol half out of his holster.

"Leave it, Lenny, please!" Dan shouted.

Lenny let the pistol slip back down into his holster.

"I don't want to hurt you, Lenny. I figure you got some good in you. But if you keep taking up for your brother, you're going to get yourself killed one day."

"We all have to die sometime," Lenny said, easily.

"Yeah, but there are a hell of a lot of things more worth dying for than Moe Tucker.

Moe sat up then and rubbed his chin.

"Sheriff," Moe said, glaring at Dan. "I want you to get this son of a bitch off my property, now."

Jones drew his pistol and pointed it at Dan. "Rankin, if you don't come along right now, I'm going to lock you up for trespassing," he said.

"What are you going to do, Sheriff, shoot me over a trespassing violation?" Dan asked.

"If I have to," Jones replied. "Come along now. You've looked at the calves and you didn't find any of yours. I've done all I can do for you."

"Yeah, I'm sure you have," Dan said. Tossing Moe's rifle to the side, he mounted his horse. "Thanks a lot for your help, Sheriff," he added sarcastically.

Lenny watched as Rankin and the sheriff rode off, then walked over to his brother. Moe was still sitting on the ground and Lenny reached out to give his brother a hand up.

Moe put his right hand in Lenny's left, but as Lenny was helping him up, he suddenly threw a whistling roundhouse right crashing into Moe's jaw. Moe went down again.

"Hey!" Moe shouted. He sat up and rubbed his jaw. "What the hell was that all about?"

"Don't you get up again, Moe," Lenny said menacingly. "If you do, I swear, I'll knock you down again."

"What's gotten into you?"

"For one thing, I don't like being lied to," Lenny said. "And for another I don't like being made part of a felony, even if it is to protect my own brother."

"I don't know what you are talking about," Moe said.

Lenny stepped up to Moe and hit him again, this time with a backhanded blow which stung, but didn't have any real chance of knocking him out.

"Cut that out!" Moe called. "What is that for?"

"I told you," Lenny said. "I don't like being lied to. Now, where are the calves you stole?"

Moe rubbed his chin again, then sighed. "They're over at the McAfees. I was going to cut you in on it, Lenny. I was going to make sure you got your share."

Lenny walked over to his horse and swung into the saddle.

"What are you going to do?"

"Nothing," Lenny said.

Moe sighed. "Good, I thought maybe you were going to do something foolish like run after Rankin and tell him."

Lenny pointed at Moe. "Moe, if you ever do anything like this again, you won't have to worry about someone coming after you."

"Why is that?" Lenny asked.

"Because, I'll kill you myself," Lenny said. He clucked to his horse and rode away.

Moe sat on the ground for a moment longer, watching Lenny disappear in the distance. Then he stood up and dusted the dirt away from the seat of his trousers.

Back in Marfa, Polly was discovering that getting a job was going to be a much more difficult task than she had thought it would be. She had applied for bookkeeping positions with most of the merchants in town, and now she was in Marfa's only bank. She was sitting in the office of Curlis Davis, president of the Texas Cattleman's Bank.

"Let me get this straight. You are applying for a position as bank clerk?" Davis asked.

"Yes."

"I must confess to a degree of curiosity, young lady. What makes you think any woman would be considered for such a position?"

"Not *any* woman. Me. I am good in mathematics and I have been trained in the art of keeping books," Polly replied. "I assure you, sir, I am perfectly qualified to be a bookkeeper, teller, or clerk, or to fill any other position a bank may offer."

"Not in my bank, you aren't," the president said resolutely. Then, seeing the expression on Polly's face, he softened his tone somewhat. "Look, miss, I don't know how it is back east, but out here, if my customers thought there was a woman involved with their money, why, they would withdraw their accounts so fast your head would swim."

"It isn't fair," Polly complained. "I'm as good as any man. I shouldn't be denied the right to make a living just because I am a woman."

"Miss, no one said life was fair," the banker replied. "Listen, do you need a job real bad?"

"Yes, I'm afraid I do. If I don't find employment, I shall soon be desperate," Polly said.

"I have a friend," he said. "You might be just what she is looking for."

"She? A woman? Who is she? Where will I find her?"

The banker held his hand out in a shushing fashion, then walked to the door of his office. He closed it, then came back to his chair.

"As I said, she is a friend of mine," he said, speaking very quietly. "She also banks with me, though her business is in Shafter."

"Shafter? Actually, I had originally planned to go on to Shafter. You say your friend banks with you?"

"Yes."

"Shafter must be an awfully small town if it doesn't even have a bank."

"Oh, it has a bank, all right, but Miss Lacoste feels that, for business reasons, it is best for her to bank here."

"Miss Lacoste? What a beautiful name. What kind of business is she in?"

"She owns a ... well ... you might call it a visiting house."

"A visiting house? You mean a hotel? A boarding-house?"

"Not exactly."

Polly looked confused. "What is it then?"

"It is a place where men come to, uh, visit women," the banker stammered. "And they pay the women for those visits."

Polly gasped. "You are talking about a bordello! Are you suggesting that I work as a prostitute?"

"No, no! Nothing like that!" the banker said quickly. "Please, don't misunderstand me, Miss Carpenter. You said you were an accountant. Miss Lacoste needs an accountant. And I assure you, her ... brothel ... as you call it, is the nicest place in Shafter."

"I don't know," Polly said. "I mean, even if I wasn't expected to be a prostitute, I don't think I could work in such a place."

"Before you turn it down, I think you should know that

Miss Lacoste confided to me that she would pay as much as one hundred dollars per month for a good bookkeeper. You are good, aren't you?"

"I'm as good as any man," Polly replied, quickly.

"Then you would be perfect for the job. If you like, I will write a letter of introduction for you."

Polly ran her hand through her hair as she thought about the proposition that had just been made to her. One hundred dollars per month was a fortune. And if this morning was any indication, the only kind of job she was likely to find in Marfa would be as a laundress or a maid.

"Are such businesses legal, here?" Polly asked. "I wouldn't want to get into trouble with the law."

"It is quite legal," the banker replied.

Why not? Polly thought. Nobody knew her out here. And if her stepfather ever came looking for her, he would never think to look for her in such a place.

"All right," she finally said. "If you would, please, write the letter for me. I shall take the train to Shafter."

"There are no trains to Shafter. You'll have to take the stage," the banker said as he began writing the letter. The banker looked at the clock on the wall. "The stage leaves in just under an hour, and it will get you there before nightfall, tonight."

Buster read the telegram then showed it to Claude. "What does it say?" Deke asked.

"You may expect delivery today," Claude read.

"It's from Deputy Gentry," Buster said. "He's tellin' us there will be money on the stagecoach."

"It ain't fair that he gets a fourth of it," Deke said. "We're the ones that's takin' all the risk."

"Yeah, but Gentry's the one that's told us where all the money is, 'n he's told us before, too," Buster said. "Him bein' a deputy sheriff like he is, means he's able to find out things like where there's money that can be stoled. And if we cut him out, we won't be gettin' no more information that we can use."

"Buster's right," Claude said. "He's give us three good ideas before 'n ever' one of 'em has worked out."

"Just like this one will," Buster said. "Come on, we need to get out there 'n be ready for the stage when it comes."

The Marfa depot of the Rio Grande Stage Company was in the corner of a feed-and-seed store. There were stacks of block salt immediately inside the door, as well as several sacks of molasses cake and rolled oats. They filled the room with a sweetly pungent smell.

Harnesses and other trapping hung from pegs on the wall, but in the corner of the building that was used as the stage depot, some effort had been made to separate it from the rest of the store. Here, there was a small counter with a window and a timetable that listed arrivals and departures to various towns in Texas.

"I'd like passage to Shafter, please," she said.

"Yes ma'am, that'll be two dollars," the ticket agent said.

"I'd like one too," a man said, coming up to the window then. When Polly turned, she gasped, for it was Doc Hawkins, the man who had come to her aid yesterday.

"Sure thing, Doc," the ticket agent said. "And to tell the truth, I know that Henry and the new marshal are going to be happy to have you ridin' with them. They're carryin' a money shipment to the Mina Grande Mine."

"The new marshal? Who is the new marshal?"

"That would be me," Will said, smiling, as he came into the depot. "The Mina Grande asked me to come over here and ride back with their money."

"Will, so you did take the job," Doc said. "Good. I hoped you would."

"It was hard to turn down," Will said. "Especially after I learned about the sweet deal you set up for my brother and me with the gambling tax."

"It's worth a tax if it keeps the games honest, and keeps the trouble down," Doc said.

"I hope everyone else feels that way about it."

"If they don't, they can find a game somewhere else," Doc replied.

"I'd better get out there," Will said, nodding toward the door. "They'll be bringing the money pouch over in a minute or two, then we'll be on our way."

Doc gave a little wave, then walked over to have a seat on a bench but when he saw that Polly was still standing and looking at him, he stood up quickly and took off his hat.

"I beg your pardon for sitting in your presence, ma'am," he said.

"Oh, no, please, sit down, sit down," she said. Quickly, she sat so that he would.

Doc pulled out a cheroot and started to light it, then he hesitated. "Do you mind, ma'am, if I smoke?" he asked.

"Go right ahead," Polly said.

Doc lit his cheroot, then folded his arms across his chest as he waited. Once or twice, Polly caught him looking at her. She knew he was trying to figure out where he had seen her.

"The stage for Shafter is ready to roll!" someone shouted and, quickly, Doc came over to pick up one of Polly's two suitcases. Archie, the coach driver, got the other. When they went outside to board the stage, Will was already up on the high seat, with a rifle across his lap.

A moment later, Archie called to the team, then snapped the whip with a loud report. The horses swung the stage around and began trotting briskly down the main street of the town.

Chapter Eight

Buster Allman, Claude Wyatt, and Deke Calhoun were
waiting at Cutback Pass. This was the ideal place to hold
up a stagecoach because while they could see the coach
as soon as it entered the pass, the three would be able to
stay out of sight until the last moment.

Then once they stopped the coach, they would have
absolute control because the pass was too narrow and
too steep to allow for any maneuvering.

"Hey, how much money is this coach s'posed to be
carryin', anyhow?" Deke asked. Buster and Claude were
both lying on their backs in the dirt, with their hands
laced behind their heads. Deke was the only one standing
and that was because he was urinating.

"I don't know, but it's got to be a lot of money or Gentry
would've never told us about it."

"You wouldn't think it, would you? I mean him bein'

a lawman 'n all, but he's give us these good ideas on who to hold up," Claude said.

Buster laughed. "Don't you know who he really is?"

"Yeah, his name is Roscoe Gentry," Claude said.

"Yeah, that's what he's called now. But when he was livin' up in Arkansas, his name was Owen Spicer. Folks used to call him The Slicer on account of the way he kilt people, by cuttin' their throats."

Buster chuckled. "It ain't a case of a lawman goin' bad. It's a case of a bad man becomin' a lawman."

"Damn. I wonder if Sheriff Jones knows that," Deke asked.

"I doubt it. There don't that many people know nothin' about it."

"How come it is that you know about it?" Claude asked.

"Owen, that is, Roscoe, is my first cousin," Buster replied.

On board the coach, Polly was looking through the window at the passing countryside, but feeling Doc's gaze on her, she looked back at him. Doc was slouched in his seat and he was holding his hands in front of him, making a tent with his fingers. His hands, Polly noticed, were well formed, and his fingers were long and supple.

"Excuse me, miss, but I have the strangest feeling we have met before," he said. Only I can't remember where and that perplexes me. Surely I would not forget such a lovely lady."

"My name is Polly Carpenter. You came to my rescue yesterday," Polly said.

For just a moment Doc looked even more confused; then a glimmer of recognition crossed his face.

"My God! You're the tenderfoot," he said.

"The same," Polly admitted. "The confusion comes from the fact that I had assumed the disguise of a man, thinking it would discourage any unwanted attention."

Doc smiled. "Well, now, that makes me feel a lot better about yesterday."

"Better? I don't understand."

"I've been asking myself ever since it happened, why I butted in. As it was a woman, and not some wet-behind-the-ears tenderfoot who was in danger, I can take comfort in the knowledge that my intrusion was completely justified."

"Not only justified, but most welcome," Polly said. "You can imagine what a shock it was to just get off the train and stumble into a situation like that. It seems that in affecting my disguise, I was nearly hoist by my own petard."

Doc laughed. "Indeed," he said. "Nevertheless, I am glad I was able to be of some service. And I will tell you that regardless of what you may have heard about the

West, here even the most ill-behaved 'boors' as I believe you called them yesterday, treat women with respect. You would have been better off by not trying to hide your true gender."

"I believe you are right," Polly replied. "I shall not commit such an error in the future."

"What brings you to Shafter, Miss Carpenter?"

"I'm going to work there, for a Miss Marie Lacoste," Polly explained.

Doc looked at her with an expression of surprise. "You're going to work for Miss Lacoste?"

"Yes. Do you know her?"

"I know her. She is a good woman," Doc said. After that, he folded his arms and looked through the window of the coach.

Polly had never met anyone quite like Doc Hawkins. He was obviously an educated man; his manner of speech indicated that. But there was something else about him. There was a private sadness just beneath the surface. She wondered what private devil plagued Doc Hawkins.

Up on the box, Will rode silently while the driver worked the horses. Archie had a name for each of his animals, and he insisted to anyone who would listen that they all recognized their own name and responded to his words. He would swear at one of them for slacking, or praise another for doing a good job. Sometimes he teased them, and he created relationships between the horses.

"Princess, look at Gilroy over there. See how he's struttin' his stuff? He's showin' out for you, Princess, what do you think of that? I know, I know, you don't like him, but we all have to work together, so try to get along, will you?"

Archie's conversation with the horses kept him so occupied that Will could be left alone with his thoughts. He wondered about the woman down in the coach. Who was she, where was she from, and why was she coming to Shafter? She obviously wasn't coming for a short visit. He could tell that from the luggage that accompanied her.

Will also thought about the money they were carrying. The pouch contained $20,000. That wasn't quite enough. But if the shipment ever got up to $100,000, he would be tempted to take the money himself. He smiled. Damn, what he and Gid could do with $100,000. They could go to San Francisco. San Francisco was a big town and he was sure there were a lot of beautiful women there. He was reasonably certain, however, that none of them could be any prettier than the girl that was riding down in the coach right now. He had no idea who she was, but she was as pretty as just about any woman he had ever seen. There was an innocence about her that greatly heightened her appeal.

Will had to get his mind back on his work. If anyone had a notion to jump the stage, the best place to do it would be at the narrows where the canyon walls squeezed in so tight that there was no room to maneuver. That was just on the other side of the double-back loop they were approaching.

Will waited for the stage to line up with the opening, which would allow him to see anyone who might be waiting for them. There! Just for an instant, he saw them. Road agents were waiting to ambush the stage! The amount of time they were exposed to view was so brief that to any but the most experienced eye, the road agents would have gone completely unnoticed. That was the advantage Will had over many other sheriffs, marshals, and shotgun guards. He had been a road agent himself, so he knew how they thought.

"Archie, they're waitin' for us on the other side," Will said. It was the first time he had spoken.

"You seen 'em for sure?"

"Yep"

"What you want me to do?"

"Just keep on driving," Will said. "I'll get Doc to go with me. We can cut across the top here while you're makin' the loop. With any luck they'll be so occupied with the stage coming that they won't notice us sneakin' up on them."

"I'll pick you up on the other side," Archie said.

Will climbed up onto the top of the stage, then leaned down to look inside. Polly was startled to see his head suddenly appear in her window as he hung upside down like a bat. She gasped.

"'Beg 'pardon, ma'am," Will said. "Doc, you want to come with me?"

Doc nodded.

Will rose back up, took his rifle, and jumped off the stage. Doc opened the door and slipped out with him.

"What's up?" Doc asked. "Someone at the narrows?"

"Yeah, three men," Will said.

Will thought that it was like Doc to know not only why he called him, but where the danger would be as well.

Will crouched low as he and Doc ran across the top of the rocks. A moment later they saw the three men. As Will had predicted, they were concentrating so intently on the stage that they didn't suspect a thing.

"Well, well," Doc called out. "Fancy seeing you boys again." They were the same three men who had accosted Polly the day before.

"What the hell? What are you doing here?" Buster yelled. At the same time he yelled, he started firing.

Will and Doc returned fire and it was all over in a matter of seconds. Buster and his two friends lay belly up in the sun.

"Did you have a run-in with those folks yesterday?" Will asked as he casually reloaded his rifle.

"Yeah," Doc said. "They were bothering Miss Carpenter."

"Miss Carpenter?"

"That's the girl in the coach," Doc said. Like Will, he had reloaded his gun and now he slipped it back into his holster.

"She's a very pretty girl," Will said. "But, if you've staked out a claim on her...."

"She's going to work for Marie Lacoste," Doc said. "Far as I know, the whole town has a claim on her."

"She's going to work for Marie?"

"Yes."

Will was surprised. He thought he knew women pretty well. He would never have guessed that the pretty, innocent-looking girl in the coach was a whore.

"These men were foolish to take a chance like this for only twenty thousand dollars," Doc said, nodding toward the bodies.

"My thoughts exactly," Will replied. "Now, if it had been a hundred thousand..."

Doc laughed. "Yes, well, Wells Fargo has considered that possibility, I'm afraid. They won't ship that much at one time without one of their own guards."

In the distance they heard the whistles and shouts of

Archie as he worked the team around the tight turn.

"Might as well put the bodies on top of the stage and take them to the next way station. Archie can make arrangements to get them taken back to Marfa for burying," Doc suggested.

"If it's all the same to you, Doc, why don't we leave them here for Sheriff Jones to worry about? No need to expose Miss Carpenter to the carcasses."

"Yes," Doc said. "I'm ashamed for not thinking of it myself. Let Jones have them."

Will walked out to the trail and flagged the stage down.

"Any trouble?" Archie asked.

"Nothing that wasn't handled," Will answered easily as he climbed back onto the box. Doc got inside and closed the door; then, with a whistle and a shout, the stage was underway again.

They were able to see Shafter for half an hour before they reached it; they were approaching it through the high country and Shafter was laid out across a treeless plateau. Seen from this angle, it was almost as if they were flying and Polly could easily imagine herself not in a stagecoach but in a balloon.

"Oh, how lonesome it looks," she said aloud.

"I beg your pardon?" Doc asked. As neither of them had spoken in quite a while, Doc wasn't sure that he had even heard her.

"It seems so lonesome," Polly repeated. "For as far as the eye can see there is nothing but emptiness, and yet, in its own, fascinating way, it is so very beautiful."

"Yes," Doc said. He quoted a few lines of poetry:

And now 'twas like all instruments,
Now like a lonely flute

"Oh! You know Coleridge!" Polly said, excitedly. She picked up the same poem.

And now it is an angel's song,
That makes the heavens be mute.

"Oh, how wonderful!" Polly said, clapping her hands happily.

"I hope I have not misled you," Doc said. He nodded toward the little town, still visible below. "I'm afraid Shafter is hardly a testimonial for the human spirit. We kill each other off on a nightly basis."

"Why, whatever do you mean, sir?" Polly asked, puzzled by Doc's statement.

"You are going to have to get used to Shafter. It's a rather wide-open town, not at all like Marfa"

Polly gasped. "Heavens, you mean it's *worse* than Marfa?" she asked, remembering the encounter with the three men who challenged her the moment she left the train.

"Well, you must remember that Marfa is a city built to serve the railroad, whereas Shafter is a new town, built upon silver. And though the population is considerably north of five hundred, it's still a town trying to find its way."

"Why are you living there?" Polly asked.

"Everyone has to be somewhere and to be honest with you, I have about exhausted all my options."

"You said Shafter was built upon silver. Is there a lot of silver there?" Polly asked.

"They've taken out more than five million dollars in the last three years," Doc said. "And the vein looks like it will continue for quite some time."

Polly let out a low whistle.

"Add the rowdy miners to the rambunctious cowboys from the surrounding ranches, mix them with whiskey, gambling, and a few soiled doves, and you can see the source of your trouble."

Polly wondered what he meant by the term *soiled doves*, but she didn't ask.

The sun was just beginning to set by the time the stage entered the town limits and rolled down the main street. Both sides of the street were lined with false-fronted buildings, with the largest being the Dust Cutter Saloon.

There were scores of men wandering up and down the street, many carrying bottles, others staggering and supporting each other to keep from falling. Some, Polly noticed, had already fallen, for there were nearly a dozen or so who were passed out, drunk in the streets.

The stage stopped in front of a three-story building. A big sign in front of the building indicated that this was the Del Rey Hotel. There were half a dozen people on the wooden porch of the hotel, and they got up to watch the stage's arrival with interest.

"Here we are, folks," Archie said as he hopped down from the front of the coach. He opened the door and helped Polly down. Will walked around to the back of the stage to take her luggage from the leather boot.

Deputy Gentry arrived just as Archie was passing the money pouch down to Harry Rutledge.

"What is that?" Gentry asked, pointing to the pouch.

"Twenty thousand dollars," Rutledge said, easily.

"Wait a minute! You had a money shipment and you didn't inform our office?"

"Why should I tell you?" Rutledge asked. "For all I know, you'd tell some of your cowboy friends and the next thing I know the money would be gone."

"Are you accusing me of stealin' your money?" Gentry asked, angrily.

"Can't very well accuse you of stealin' any money now,

can I, Deputy?" Rutledge replied. He held up the money pouch. "Seein' as I have the money right here."

Gentry blinked his eyes, not sure if he was being maligned or not. "Yes, well, just remember this. Anytime the coach is outside of the town limits, it's in the jurisdiction of the county sheriff's office." Making a fist, he pointed to his chest with his thumb. "I'm the county sheriff's deputy, which means if anything had happened to it, me 'n the sheriff, would a' been responsible."

"You would have been responsible. Yes, that was sort of my idea, as well," Rutledge said, and Doc laughed. "But you needn't have worried. It was well-guarded."

"By who?"

"By Doc Hawkins and me," Will said.

"How can you guard it? You have no jurisdiction outside the town limits."

"He was acting as Archie's shotgun guard," Rutledge said. "That's all the jurisdiction he needs." Rutledge looked at Archie. "Did you boys have any trouble?" he asked.

"Nothing we couldn't handle," Archie answered. "Three men tried to hold us up, but Will and Doc left them dead, out on the trail."

"At Cutback Pass?" Rutledge asked.

"Yes."

"The dumb bastards always try it there. You'd think, by now, everyone would know better," Rutledge said.

The information that three men had been killed on the trail was a surprise to Polly. No one had mentioned anything about it to her.

"Are you telling me you just left three dead men out on the trail?" Gentry asked.

"That's county jurisdiction," Will said. "We figured we would leave them for you."

"And just what am *I* supposed to do with them?" Gentry sputtered angrily.

"I don't know, it's like you said, Gentry, you're the deputy, so somethin' like this would be up to the sheriff, I reckon. So, you can just bring 'em in, or let the buzzards have 'em," Will said. "It makes no difference to me."

"Will you be staying here at the hotel, miss?" Archie asked Polly. "If so, I'll have your luggage carried inside.

"No, she'll be staying with me," Marie interjected, arriving at that moment.

There was a collective gasp from more than a dozen men when they heard that Polly would be staying with Marie. The thought of this beautiful young woman being a whore caused half of them to start planning their next visit to Carnation House.

"You are Polly Carpenter, aren't you?" Marie asked.
"Yes."

"I thought so. Mr. Davis telegraphed me that you would be arriving on the stage. But he neglected to say how beautiful you are. You will be working with me. I am Marie Lacoste."

Marie's greeting was so warm and genuine that she won Polly over right away. She stuck her hand out and Polly shook it.

"I am pleased to meet you," she said. "But I would be perfectly willing to stay in the hotel. I wouldn't want to put you out."

"Nonsense, you wouldn't be putting me out at all. Besides, you'll find my place much nicer than the hotel, I promise you. And free lodging comes with the job."

"In that case, I will be happy to stay with you," Polly said.

"Ralph, do be a dear, would you, and carry Miss Carpenter's bags down to the Carnation House?" Marie said to one of the men.

"I'd be proud to," Ralph answered. He took the two suitcases from Will, then started down the street toward a large white Victorian house. Compared to every other building in town, the house looked like a mansion.

"Oh, my, is that where you live?" Polly asked, pointing toward the house.

"Yes, that's the Carnation House. It's where you will live as well. Welcome home," Marie said.

Chapter Nine

"Someone tried to hold up the stagecoach," Gentry told Sheriff Jones when he returned to the sheriff's office.

"Tried to? What happened?"

"Them that tried was killed by Will Crockett and Doc Hawkins."

"Damn, you mean both of them was on the stage at the same time?"

"Yeah. Crockett was hired by the stagecoach company to be the shotgun guard for this trip 'n as it turns out, Doc Hawkins warn't nothin' more 'n a passenger who was comin' back from a trip he took."

Sheriff Jones chuckled. "That sure was bad luck for whoever it was tried to hold up the stage wasn't it? I mean what with Crockett 'n Doc Hawkins both on the stage."

"Yeah," Gentry said. "It was bad luck. Oh, by the way, Carnation House got a new whore."

"A new one, huh? Marie must be doin' just real good for herself."

"You know what I was thinkin'?" Gentry asked.

"No, what?"

"I was thinkin' maybe we ought to put some sort of tax on that whore house, somethin' like a dollar a day for each one of the whores she's got workin' there."

Sheriff Jones shook his head. "No, that won't work. Neither the mayor nor the city council would approve it."

Gentry smiled. "Only, this wouldn't be a city tax, this would be a county tax, 'n seein' as you're the highest official in the county, why you would be the one puttin' on the tax."

"Yeah," Sheriff Jones said with a broad smile. "I could do that, couldn't I?"

When Gentry returned to his desk, he started figuring the proceeds they would get from the new tax. It worked out to three hundred sixty dollars per month that he and the sheriff could split. Not like the money he had planned to haul in from the stagecoach hold up, but under the circumstances, this was better than nothing at all. And this was legal, not that being legal mattered to him

Five thousand dollars, Gentry thought. Will Crockett and Doc Hawkins had cost him five thousand dollars. Not only that, they killed the men he had working for him.

Now he would have to get some new men and train them to do exactly what he told them to do.

He knew that before he got anyone new, he would have to get rid of Crockett and Hawkins. But how would he do that? He didn't know anyone good enough to face Doc Hawkins, except ironically, perhaps Crockett. But that wasn't likely, as Will Crockett and Doc Hawkins had become friends.

But in reality, it wasn't a matter of facing them down. He didn't want a reputation earned by killing either of them in a fair gunfight. All he wanted was for Crockett and Hawkins to be dead. Surely he could find some way for that to happen.

When Polly opened her eyes the next morning she lay with her head on the pillow for a moment or two, wondering where she was. A bright splash of sunlight spilled in through the open window, showing wallpaper that featured a repeating design of baskets of blue flowers.

"Mary! Mary, you get those clothes hung up on the line, do you hear me?"

"Yes, Mama," a young girl's voice answered.

The voices came from outside. They drifted into the room on the soft breeze which filled the muslin curtains and lifted them out over the rose-colored carpet.

Polly heard the little girl singing a cheery morning

song and when she raised her head to look outside, she discovered that she was looking down onto an alley. The little girl was hanging wash on the line in the back yard of the house just across the alley behind the Carnation House. Polly sat up, wondering what time it was. From the position of the sun she knew that it must be fairly late in the morning. She didn't normally sleep this late, but she decided she must have been exceptionally tired from the trip the day before. Also, the town, which had been so noisy last night, was very quiet this morning.

Polly dressed, then went out into the hallway. She saw an old Mexican woman folding towels and sheets and stacking them on shelves in a hall closet. She had never seen so many towels before and she wondered how one place could use so many.

A door opened just across the hall from Polly's room and a pretty young woman stepped out. Polly looked at the young woman in some surprise because not only was she pretty, she was also totally naked.

"Teresa, I ran out of towels last night," the naked girl said. She had long, luxuriant black hair and she brushed her hand through it to push the strands back away from her face.

"I'm sorry," Teresa said. "Please excuse." She gave the young woman a handful of towels. The young woman looked at Polly and smiled. "You must be Polly," she said.

"Yes," Polly answered, puzzled at how the girl knew her name.

"I'm Lucy," the girl said. She extended her hand and Polly shook it, trying to act as if there was nothing at all unusual in her shaking hands with a naked woman. Lucy laughed. "Last night after you got in, Marie told us all about you."

"How many of you are there?"

"Twelve," Lucy said. "Most of 'em sleep all day and don't come out until late afternoon. I'd be asleep myself, but I had an all-night visitor."

"A visitor?"

"A customer," Lucy said.

"Oh."

Lucy laughed. "Marie said you weren't really going to be one of us. By that, I mean, you don't plan to...uh... be with any of the men."

"No. I think I'm just supposed to be a bookkeeper."

"Marie said that she wanted all of us to accept you as part of the family. Well, I don't think we'll have any trouble accepting you as our sister, but the question is, will you be able to accept us?"

"I ... I think so. I don't know. I've never really been in this kind of a situation before, but I'm certainly going to try."

To Polly's surprise, Lucy laughed. "At least you're

125

honest about it. I'll talk to all the others about you. If we try hard enough, I think we can win you over."

Gid was in the Hermitage eating breakfast when a shadow fell across his table and he looked up to see a tall, bearded man, wearing a badge.

"You Gid Crockett?"

Gid was instantly alert. He had never seen this man before, but the badge he was wearing was stamped, U.S. Marshal. Was he after Gid? Under the table, Gid put his hand on his pistol.

"I'm Gid Crockett," he said.

"I'm Ephraim Weaver, U.S. Marshal," the tall man said. "I looked for your brother this morning, but I couldn't find him. Someone told me you would be having breakfast over here."

Gid eased the pistol out of its holster and waited for the U.S. Marshal to make his move.

"You and your brother are the town marshals of Shafter, aren't you?"

"Yes."

"I've got a job I would like you to do. Of course, I'd have to swear you in as a deputy U.S. Marshal." He reached for one of Gid's biscuits. "Do you mind? I haven't had breakfast."

"No, help yourself," Gid said, relieved that this apparently wasn't what he thought it was going to be. He let his pistol slide back down into its holster, then held up his hand to get the attention of the waiter. "Louis, bring us some more biscuits, would you, please?" he called. "And maybe another bowl of gravy?"

Ephraim used the biscuit plate as his own, and he spooned the rest of the gravy over the biscuits. "I'm looking for some mules," he said, as he picked up a fork and started to help himself. "U.S. Army mules. Two of them."

"Do you have any idea where these mules might be?"

"Yeah, I know exactly where they are."

"Well, then there's no problem. Just go get them."

"They're on the Tucker ranch," Ephraim said.

"The Tuckers stole some mules from the army?"

"No, they didn't steal them," Ephraim said. "Fact is, they bought 'em, fair and proper. But the fella they bought 'em from stole 'em. That means they're still U.S. Army property. The Tuckers have to give them back."

Gid chuckled. "From what I know of the Tuckers, I don't think they're going to want to do that."

"So, you do know them?"

"Yes, I know them," Gid said.

"If I ride out there and ask them to return the mules, will they do it?" Ephraim asked.

"I doubt it. But if Lenny is there, he might talk the others out of killing you."

127

"That's what I was afraid of. That's why I want to make you and your brother my deputies. I thought maybe the three of us, along with Sheriff Jones and his deputy, would present a formidable enough force that we might be able to get the mules back with no trouble."

"You've asked Jones and Gentry and they have agreed to go?"

"I haven't asked them yet."

"Don't bother," Gid said. "The Tuckers have the sheriff and his deputy in their hip pocket." Abruptly, he stood up. "Let's go," he said.

"Go? Go where?"

"Out to the Tucker ranch to get the mules. Isn't that what this is all about?"

"What about your brother?"

"He had all the fun on the stagecoach hold up, it's my time now."

"You're saying just the two of us?"

"Yeah. That is, unless you don't want to go."

The U.S. Marshal smiled. "You really are full of piss and vinegar, aren't you? All right, Crockett, let's go."

It was a good half-hour ride to the Double T Ranch. Gid had never been to the Tucker spread before and he had been wanting to see it. This gave him an excuse.

The ranch first came into view when they topped an

overlook; they sat on their horses and looked down at the spread. Cibolo Creek swept around the ranch, giving it a year-round supply of water and making it the most valuable piece of land in the entire valley.

Even though Gid had found himself in the opposite camp from the Tuckers, he felt an immediate affinity for the ranch and could understand why they would fight to protect it. If someone had come up to him at that moment and offered him the Mina Grande silver mine or the Tucker ranch, he would have taken the ranch. The silver would eventually be all mined out, but the ranch would go on forever.

"You ready?" Ephraim asked, interrupting Gid's reverie.

"Ready," Gid replied.

"Let's do it."

Gid took a deep breath, then slapped his legs against the side of his horse to urge him forward. For a moment he wished he had not been so hasty in leaving Will behind.

They passed under a gate which featured a set of polished longhorn steer horns, then rode up to the front of the house. By the time they got there, Moe Tucker was standing on the front porch, cradling a shotgun.

"Mr. Tucker?" Ephraim said, touching the brim of his hat. He pointed to the shotgun in Tucker's hands. "Holding a shotgun like that doesn't seem very neighborly."

"You're city law, ain't you? City law's got no business out here."

"I'm a United States marshal," Ephraim Weaver said. "For the purposes of this visit, I have deputized Mr. Crockett."

"Whether you deputized him or not, he is still city law. Maybe you don't know it, but us Tuckers ain't been gettin' along none too good with the townfolk, especially the town law. So, I'd say your comin' out here ain't bein' too neighborly."

"Mr. Tucker, could we get down and talk for a while?"

"I can hear you just fine, right where you are," Moe said.

"All right, if you say so," Ephraim replied. "Mr. Tucker, did you come into a pair of mules, recently?"

"I reckon I did. What's it to you?"

"They belong to the U.S. Army, Mr. Tucker. I'm here to take them back."

The shotgun had been broken open at the breech, but now Moe snapped it shut with an ominous click. He didn't raise the barrel, but the threat had been implied, nevertheless.

"You tryin' to tell me I stole them mules?" Moe asked.

"No, sir, not at all," Ephraim said. "I know that you bought the mules from a man named Coleman Patterson."

"Well, I don't understand. If you're admittin' I didn't steal 'em, how can they still belong to the army?"

"Because the mules weren't Patterson's to sell," Ephraim explained.

"Seems to me, then, that this is a matter betwixt the army and Mr. Patterson. Don't see how it affects me."

"It affects you, Mr. Tucker, because you have the mules and they still belong to the army."

"The hell they do. You said yourself I bought them mules. They belong to me now."

"Mr. Tucker, under the law, you are technically guilty of larceny, just as if you had stolen the mules yourself," Ephraim explained. "You see, you are guilty of receiving stolen goods. I could arrest you, but I won't. The army is willing to offer a deal. No charges will be brought if you'll return the mules."

"I can't see returnin' what was bought and paid for."

"Like I told you, they weren't Patterson's to sell. Consider this, Tucker. Suppose someone went to Marfa and sold some of your cattle, then the man who bought the cattle came out here with the receipt and wanted to cut out a hundred head or so. Would you give him his cattle? He bought the cows, and he has the receipt to prove it."

"I don't give a damn about the receipt. He didn't buy the cows unless he bought them from me," Moe growled.

"Well, Tucker, you have just made my point," Weaver said. "The receipt you have with Patterson is no good either. The mules still belong to the army."

Moe stood there, holding the shotgun pointed at Gid and Marshal Weaver for a long moment. Finally, with a sigh, he broke open the shotgun and extracted the two shells, then leaned the empty weapon against the front of the house.

"Never let it be said that Moe Tucker wouldn't cooperate with the law," he said. "'Tell the truth, I don't know why I bought the worthless critters in the first place. Take the damned things. They ain't done nothin' from the day I brought 'em in but eat, anyway. I'll go to the barn and get 'em and bring 'em to you, and good riddance."

"Crockett," Ephraim said quietly, after Tucker left.

"Yes?"

"There's someone around the corner of the house." Ephraim got off his horse and began adjusting the bridle. Then, moving quickly, he pulled his gun, dropped, and rolled toward the corner. He was lying prone with his gun out and pointed toward the person behind the corner, before anyone knew he was about to make his move.

"Come on out from there," Ephraim called.

Gid looked toward the corner and saw Lenny Tucker stepping out from behind the building with his hands up, hesitantly. He was wearing a gun.

"What were you doin' back there, mister?" Ephraim asked. "Plannin' on shootin' us in the back once we got the mules?"

"No," Lenny said. "I was just listening to what was going on, that's all."

"Why didn't you come 'round front?"

"I didn't want to interfere."

"Shuck out of that gun."

"Marshal," Lenny said, his face growing red in anger. "Don't make me do that. This is my ranch; these are my men. If you make me drop my gun, it'll make me look bad in front of them."

"I can't worry about that none. Shuck out of that gun."

"Marshal let him keep his gun," Gid said. "I don't think he means us any harm."

Weaver shook his head, no. "My motto is, it's better to be safe than sorry," he explained.

"Don't make him do this," Gid said. "No need to bring shame on the man. After all, they didn't steal the mules. They paid good money, thinkin' they were buyin' them."

Ephraim looked at Gid, then back toward Lenny. "All right," he said. "You can keep your gun, mister. But I aim to keep an eye on you."

"Crockett?" Lenny said.

"Yeah?"

"Thanks."

Moe Tucker returned then, leading two mules. He handed the ropes to Ephraim.

"The halters 'n rope belong to me. I'd be obliged to

have 'em back when you're done with 'em."

"I'll see to it, Mr. Tucker, and I appreciate your coop-eration," Ephraim said. He clucked at his horse as he and Gid started back down the road.

Moe and Lenny stood there for a moment, watching as Gid and the U.S. Marshal rode off.

"Why didn't you kill the bastards when you had the chance?" Moe snorted in disgust.

"You would've liked that, wouldn't you?" Lenny replied.

"Damn right I would have liked it. It would have made a man out of you."

"They were only doin' their job."

"Yeah, well, I got a feelin' that the time is comin' when there's goin' to be a showdown between us and them two new town marshals," Moe said. "And they'll just be doin' their job when it happens. I wonder if I'll be able to count on you?"

"I hope it won't ever come to that," Lenny said. "But if it does, you'll find me standin' right there beside you."

Chapter Ten

In the hopes of improving relationships between the citizens of Shafter and the ranchers, cowhands and miners from the surrounding area, the town of Shafter decided to sponsor a spring square dance. In a meeting in the conference room at the Del Rey Hotel, the Shafter Square Dance Delegation, consisting of the town council, the merchants' council, and the Ladies' Civics and Betterment Committee had a spirited debate as to whether or not to issue an invitation to Moe Tucker and Isaac and Amos McAfee.

The Ladies Civics and Betterment Committee argued against it, insisting that if they showed up there would only be trouble. But the merchants' council reminded them that the entire purpose of the dance was to try and mend fences, and if they didn't let Moe and the McAfees attend they would accomplish nothing. Reluctantly, the town council agreed and the dance committee voted to extend invitations to both the Tucker and the McAfee ranches.

"What about Marie Lacoste and the ladies who work for her?" Mayor J.C. Malone asked.

Upon hearing the mayor's suggestion, Mrs. Emma Holloway, chairwoman of the Civics and Betterment Committee, pulled her considerable frame up from the chair and, sliding her spectacles up her nose, glared at the mayor. "Absolutely not!" Mrs. Holloway snarled. "In the first place, they are not ladies, they are prostitutes, and in the second place I am shocked that you would even suggest such a thing!"

"Well I suggested it, Mrs. Holloway, because you can't very well have a dance without women.

"I assure you, sir, there will be women at the dance," Mrs. Holloway said. "Our entire committee will attend, provided you don't make our attendance impossible by bringing in all the dregs of our society."

"I meant young ... uh ... single women," Malone said, correcting himself quickly. "Most of the ladies of our town are married, whereas most of the young men who will be attending are single. We should provide them with someone to dance with."

"I will not countenance any activity that supplies whores to the cowboys," Emma said, and the other ladies applauded her.

"All right, then, what about the new girl Marie has working for her?" Jackson asked. "What is her name?"

"Polly Carpenter," Harry Rutledge answered.

"I am shocked that you would even know the name of any woman who works there," Emma said.

"Miss Carpenter is not one of Miss Lacoste's girls," Rutledge said. "She is a bookkeeper only."

"Then that settles it—we will invite Miss Carpenter," Mayor Malone said, ending the discussion.

"And now, there is the question of our two new lawmen," someone said.

"No, there isn't question. The Crockett brothers will be invited."

"Those men rode with Quantrill during the war. There is no telling how much blood is on their hands. How could we possibly invite them to the social event of the year?"

"We have pinned badges on those men and asked them to put their lives on the line for us," Mayor Malone said in spirited defense. "This is not even a matter for debate. They *will* be invited ... and that is the end of it."

At the same time the dance committee was meeting to discuss who to include, and more important, whom to exclude from their invitation list, Gid Crockett was in the marshal's office, just down the street from the Del Rey Hotel. He was playing a game of solitaire at the desk when Dan Rankin came in.

"Marshal, can I talk to you?" Dan asked.

"Actually, I'm the deputy, not the marshal, but go ahead," Gid said. Gid needed a red seven, and, peeking into the deck, found one. He played it on the black eight.

"Can you get a card out of the deck like that?" Dan asked, momentarily distracted by Gid's cheating.

"Why the hell not? I'm playing myself," Gid answered, easily.

Dan chuckled. "I guess you have a point."

"If you're here about your calves, there's nothing we can do about them," Gid said.

"You know about the calves?"

"Everybody knows about them," Gid said. He turned up an ace.

"Then you know they were stolen."

"Yep. And I know Jones took you out to the Double T to look for them. You didn't find anything, did you?"

"No. They weren't there," Dan said. "But I just found out they never were there. They're over at the McAfee place."

"How do you know?"

"One of Slim's pards rides for the Rocking J spread. He was over at the Bar M Bar ranch last week and saw a pen full of un-branded calves. He had seen ours after we got them rounded up, and he's sure he recognized some of them. The McAfee's stole my cows."

"I wouldn't be surprised," Gid said as he continued to play cards.

"Well?" Dan said in an exasperated voice.

"Well what?"

"Well, I want you to go after them," Dan said. "I told you, they are my cows. I want them back."

Will had come into the conversation in time to overhear enough of it to know what it was about. He answered for Gid.

"We can't go get those calves for you, Rankin," he said.

"Why the hell not? They're my calves. I'll admit that the McAfees probably have their brands on them by now, but they're my calves. And everyone who works on my ranch will testify to that fact."

"I'm not disputing that they are your calves," Will said. "I'm just telling you we've got no authority to go get them back for you, that's all."

"You're wearin' badges ain't you?"

Will chuckled and looked down at the star that was pinned to his shirt.

"Yeah," he answered. "Who would've ever thought that the Crocketts would be wearing badges? But as far as your cows are concerned, these badges are worthless pieces of tin. We're the law only from the backside of the Jingle Bob Corral to the other side of Seth Rupert's outhouse. Go one foot beyond either one and commit a crime and all we can do is watch you do it."

"Yeah, well, that ain't the way I heard it," Dan said, bitterly. He pointed to Gid. "I heard you went out to the Double T and brought back a couple of mules for the army."

"Word does get around here, doesn't it?" Gid asked.

"Well, did you go out there for a couple of mules, or not?"

"Yes, I did."

"All right, so tell me, Deputy Crockett, how is it that you can bring back mules for the army, but you can't help me recover my calves?"

"Because I was deputized, that day, by a U.S. Marshal to go with him to get the mules," Gid said. "But it was only a temporary thing. I'm not a deputy U.S. Marshal anymore."

"Then you're telling me there's nothing I can do about it?"

"There's nothing legal, that you can do," Gid replied.

"What do you mean, nothing legal?"

"They're your calves aren't they?" Gid said. "Hell, if they were mine, I'd ride out there and get them back."

"Are you tellin' me to break the law?" Rankin asked.

"Why the hell not?" Gid replied, easily, as he looked for a black nine by rifling through the deck. "It's not our law."

The Shafter Spring Square Dance took place in the ball-room of the Del Rey Hotel. It was held on a Saturday night and from late afternoon on, ranchers and their wives and cowboys and miners began arriving in town. Many came into town in wagons and buckboards carrying their entire families. It was the daughters of the ranchers and businessmen of the town, some as young as fourteen, who made up the cortege of single women available for the cowboys and miners.

For the most part the ranchers were at their best. With their wives and children along, none of the ranch-ers were anxious for any trouble, and the cowboys and miners, aware that their jobs might depend upon their own good behavior, also managed to put their best foot forward. The townspeople put their hostility toward the ranchers aside for the duration of the ball, and some of them even managed to smile and wave at the wagons and buckboards as they arrived.

By dusk the excitement which had been steadily building around the ballroom of the Del Rey Hotel was full blown. The musicians could be heard practicing, and children were gathered around the glowing windows to peek inside. The dance floor had been cleared of tables and chairs and the band was installed on the platform at the front of the room.

Even though not everyone was there, the band reached

such a point of fine tuning that they were no longer able to hold back. They plunged into their first song, "Buffalo Gals." After that came "Little Joe the Wrangler" and then "The Gandy Dancers' Ball."

By now, horses and buggies were beginning to pile up on the street in front of the hotel. Every hitching post was full and the large lot at the Jingle Bob Corral was crammed with buckboards and wagons. Men and women were streaming along the board sidewalks headed for the hotel—the women in colorful gingham, the men in clean blue denims. Many of them sported brightly decorated vests as well.

There was one other invited guest who required some discussion by the dance committee before they issued her invitation. Although neither Marie, nor any of the girls who worked for her would be welcome at the dance, the dance committee had decided that Polly Carpenter could attend. By now everyone knew that though she was employed by the Carnation House, she wasn't one of the soiled doves. And, as she was an unmarried and very pretty young woman, they knew that her presence would be an attraction to single young men.

When Polly began questioning the other girls about what one should wear to such dances, and what they were like, she learned that there had never been one prior to this one, so there was no precedent. She was also surprised to discover that none of the other girls had received an invitation to this one.

"I don't understand," she said. "Are you telling me that none of you received an invitation? But, why not? Why, it's the only subject of conversation in town right now. Surely the invitations have merely been misplaced. I can't believe that you were not invited."

"Polly, think about it," Lucy said. "The wives and daughters of the town folk will be there tonight. Even the kids. We wouldn't be welcome."

"But, that's awful," Polly protested. "Don't people even give you a chance? Don't they take the time to know you, to see how nice all of you really are?"

Lucy laughed. "Polly, didn't you say you came from Memphis?"

"Yes."

"Did you know any of our kind in Memphis?"

"By, 'our kind' you mean soiled doves?"

"Yes. Did you know any?"

"No."

"I didn't think so. Now, back in Memphis, if you were at a party for your family and friends and several prostitutes suddenly made an appearance, would you have accepted them with open arms?"

Polly looked at Lucy for a moment, then she smiled, sheepishly.

"No," she was forced to admit. "I'm afraid I would not have. I'm sorry."

"Don't apologize, honey. That is just the way things are. We know it, and we don't hold it against anyone, not even the ladies of this town."

"All right. If none of you can go, then I won't go either," Polly said. "After all, I am one of you. I may not be a soiled dove, but I feel that you are all my friends, my sisters."

"Please, you must go," Daisy insisted.

"No, I wouldn't hear of it."

"But, don't you understand? If you go, then it's as if a little piece of us is going as well. You must go and look at everything and remember everything so that when you come back, you can tell us all about it."

"Daisy is right," Lucy said. "If you go, it'll be a little like all of us are going."

Polly looked at Marie, and Marie smiled. "They're quite serious, Polly," she said. "We do want you to go, for all of us."

"All right," Polly said. "I feel bad about being the only one of us who can go, but I'll go."

Lucy smiled. "Thank you for saying 'the only one of us'. That means that you really are one of us."

"Well of course I am," Polly said, as she hugged Lucy, then each of the other girls as they gathered around her.

The dance had already started by the time Polly left Carnation House for the walk to the Del Rey Hotel. She could hear the high skirling of the fiddle almost as soon as she was on the street. Under the music was the sound of laughter and the shuffling of feet, and the lilting voice of the dance-caller.

Will Crockett was standing at the front door, and when Polly arrived, he tipped his hat.

"Good evening, Miss Carpenter," he said.

"Good evening, Marshal."

"Perhaps you would do me the honor of a dance later this evening?"

"Yes, I would be pleased to," Polly replied.

The light and sound that had spilled through the doors were but a tiny bit of the brightly swirling excitement going on inside. Here and there, bright pinpoints of light flashed from beneath an ear, or in the hollow of the neck as a diamond or ruby or emerald caught the golden light from the many candles and kerosene lanterns that were scattered about.

"Grab your partners 'n form your squares!" the caller shouted.

The men started toward the young women. For just a moment Polly thought she would be left out—then she saw Will, smiling broadly, coming toward her. He claimed her, and they moved into one of the squares.

The music began with the fiddles loud and clear, the guitars carrying the rhythm, and the accordion providing the counterpoint. The caller began to shout. He laughed and clapped his hands and stomped his feet and danced around on the platform in compliance with his own calls, bowing and whirling as if he had a girl and was in one of the squares himself. The dancers moved and swirled to the caller's commands.

"Circle eight and you'll go straight,
    Then all go east on a westbound freight,
    Push over Sal and a pick up Kate,
    Then all join hands and circle eight.
    Swing your partner 'round and 'round,
    And turn your corner upside down.
    And turn your corner like swingin' on a gate,
    And meet your partner for a grand chain eight."

Around the dance floor sat those who were without partners looking on wistfully, and those who were too old, holding back those who were too young. At the punch bowl table, cowboys added so much of their own alcoholic ingredients to the punch that though many drank from the bowl, the contents never seemed to diminish.

The dance finished and Polly fanned herself and smiled at Will. Her face was covered with a patina of perspiration and a curl of hair stuck to her forehead.

She blew a stream of air across her face and the lock of hair was dislodged.

A couple of the cowboys got into an argument over the attentions of one of the girls and they were glaring and growling at each other, though cooler heads prevailed, and the argument was settled without Will taking a hand in it.

"I saw your brother," Polly said. "He was in the kitchen over at the Carnation House. I think Señor Munoz was cooking something special for him, tonight."

"Gid isn't much for dancing," Will answered. "But he does like to eat."

A shy, young cowboy asked Polly to dance then, and she obliged him. She danced with three others, then again with Will, then with a young miner, then again with Will.

Will, she noticed, had not danced with any of the other women, though Polly saw several of them looking toward him with open invitation in their eyes. The fact that he did dance with her, and was there for her between her dances, gave her a sense of proprietorship that she rather enjoyed.

One of the men she danced with was Lenny Tucker, though she felt a little guilty dancing with him because she knew that Lucy liked him.

"I'm only dancing with you as Lucy's surrogate," Polly told him.

"As her what?" Lenny asked.

Polly laughed. "That means I'm standing in for Lucy, since she isn't here to dance with you herself."

"Yes, how come she isn't here? Knowing Lucy, I would have thought she would really enjoy something like this."

Polly smiled and pretended that she didn't understand what Lenny meant, but in fact, she did know, because she knew that Lenny was one of Lucy's most regular customers.

A few dances after she had been with Lenny, Moe Tucker came over to her. As she was standing with Will Crockett, Moe spoke to him first.

"Good evenin', Marshal Crockett," he said. He pulled his jacket open to show that he wasn't armed. "As you can see, I'm not wearin' a gun. What do you say me and you call a truce for tonight?"

"All right by me."

"I promised my brother, Lenny, I would be on my best behavior, and I aim to keep that promise."

"Good. Then we shouldn't have any trouble tonight, should we?"

Moe looked at Polly. "I seen you dancin' with my brother, a while ago, Miss Carpenter. And I'm figurin', why would you settle for Lenny, when you could have me? How about a dance?"

Polly looked toward Will with an expression of alarm on her face.

Moe, misunderstanding her look, added, "That is, if the marshal don't mind."

"Miss Carpenter is her own person," Will said. "She doesn't need my permission. On the other hand, she doesn't have to dance with you if she doesn't want to," he added, pointedly.

That was what Polly wanted to hear, for the truth was she had no wish whatsoever to dance with Moe Tucker. She had heard too much about him from Marie and the other girls at the Carnation House, and none of what she had heard was good.

"Thank you for the invitation," Polly said. "But I think I'll pass."

"Why not? You danced with Lenny. Ain't I good enough for you? Or, bein' as you work over at the whorehouse, maybe you only dance with them that visit the whorehouse on a regular basis."

"Miss Carpenter doesn't need a reason why she doesn't want to dance with you, Tucker," Will said. "She said no, and that's it. Now, move on."

Moe glared at the two of them with such intensity that it frightened Polly, and she took an involuntary step toward Will.

"Miss Carpenter, would you care to get a breath of fresh air?" Will invited.

"Yes," Polly answered. "Yes, I would like that very

much. Thank you."

It was cooler outside, and half a dozen other couples were also taking advantage of the night air.

"Oh, could we take a walk?" Polly asked.

"All right," Will agreed.

They walked the entire length of the boardwalk until they reached the edge of town, then continued on for another hundred yards or so until the sound and the lights of the town were behind them. Now the music from the dance was barely audible. They heard a woman's scream, not of fear obviously, for it was followed immediately by her laughter, which carried clearly above everything.

Ahead of them lay the Chinati Mountains, great slabs of black and silver in the soft wash of moonlight.

"Oh, look at that," Polly said. "I had no idea that anything this wild and rugged could be so beautiful."

"It is pretty, all right," Will agreed.

"Marshal ... "

"Why don't you call me Will? To tell the truth, I'm still not quite used to being a lawman. And I sure don't like being reminded of it every time a pretty woman opens her mouth."

"All right, Will," Polly said with a smile. "But Marie says that you and your brother are good lawmen."

"So Marie has my brother and me all figured out, does she? What else does she say?"

"She says that you rode with Quantrill. Did you?"

"Yes, we did."

"What a magnificent adventure that must've been!" Polly said in awe. "I remember my father saying that Quantrill was a true champion of the South and that anyone who rode with him was a hero."

"There are those who would disagree with you," Will said. "Some would say that we used the Confederate flag as the authority to plunder and murder."

"But, that's not true, is it?"

"I can't deny it out of hand," Will said. "Truth is, I'm not all that proud of everything I've done in my life," Will said, quietly. He touched the star that was pinned to his shirt. "Even this," he added. "I'm a lawman in name only. I don't have the slightest idea of how to go about being a marshal. Dan Rankin, who is a good man even though he is a rancher, came to Gid and me for help, and there was nothing we could do for him. There's a big showdown coming between the townspeople and the ranchers ... or at least the Tuckers and the McAfees, and there's nothing Gid and I can do to stop it."

"Who is in the wrong?" Polly asked.

"What do you mean?"

"The ill will that exists between the town and the ranchers. Someone is right, and someone is wrong. Who is in the wrong?"

Will laughed. "It's easy to see that you're new out here," he said. "You always assume that someone is right, and someone is wrong."

"Why shouldn't I make such an assumption? It certainly makes it easier to solve the problem. All you have to do is go to the person who is in the wrong, make it right."

"You think it is that simple, huh?" Will asked. "Well, I wish that were so. But in this case there's enough wrong to go around for everyone. However, if all things were added up, I would guess that most of the wrong would belong to the Tuckers and the McAfees. They're the ones who seem to be keeping everything stirred up. And, if you want my opinion, it's because they're trying to cover up for the fact that they are throwing a long rope."

"Throwing a long rope? What does that mean?"

"It means they're doing a little rustling," Will said. "There's no doubt in my mind that Dan Rankin is right when he says they stole his cattle. In addition, the Tuckers and the McAfees are just downright mean."

Polly shook her head. "No, that's not true," she said. "At least, not for Lenny Tucker. He isn't at all like the others. He has always been the perfect gentleman around me, and Marie and Lucy think he is very nice."

"Don't be too taken in by him," Will suggested.

"Why? Do you know something about him that I don't know?"

"No, but I have known men like him. They seem like nice, quiet men, but they're the kind who can be the most dangerous."

"But he really is different from his brother," Polly insisted. "I haven't heard anyone say one good thing about Moe, but everyone talks about Lenny's good qualities."

"Just remember this. One of the strongest 'good' qualities is loyalty," Will said. "Everybody admires loyalty. But absolute loyalty blinds you to everything else. If Moe brings things to a head, you can bet that Lenny will be right there with him. He may not want to, but in the end his loyalty to his brother will be so strong that he can't do anything else."

"Oh," Polly said, as if getting an insight at that moment. "I understand what you are talking about, now. That's how it was with you and Quantrill, wasn't it?"

"What do you mean?"

"You said you weren't all that proud of everything you did ... but you did it anyway. It was because of your loyalty to him."

"Yes," Will admitted. "That's pretty smart of you," he added. "I hadn't thought about it like that before, but that's exactly the way it was."

"You *had* thought about it," Polly said. "That's why you know so much about Lenny's situation. You just hadn't applied it to yourself before, that's all."

They stopped walking then, and Polly looked back toward the town, now a glowing cluster of buildings on the desert floor.

"Look how far we have come. I had no idea," she said.

"Yeah, I guess we had better start back, unless we want to wind up wandering, like Moses in the desert," Will suggested.

"I wonder why he wasn't there tonight," Polly said as they started back toward the hotel.

"You wonder why who wasn't there tonight?"

"Dan Rankin. Neither he, nor any of his men were there. Don't you find that a little strange?"

"Well, there's bad blood between Rankin and the Tuckers and the McAfees. I guess he just didn't want to be around them."

Chapter Eleven

From the opposite end of town, unnoticed by Will and Polly, Roscoe Gentry rode in, his horse moving at a brisk trot. He tied the horse off just in front of the hotel, then went in. Standing just inside the door for a moment, he saw Moe Tucker and Isaac and Amos McAfee leaning against the wall behind the punch table, all of whom were holding a glass of the drink which, by now, was a concoction that only the most determined drinker could stomach. He started over toward them.

"Hey, Deputy," a cowboy called out from near the punch bowl. "Where you been? You've damn near missed all the fun. You're 'bout a day late and a dollar short for all the doin's."

Gentry looked at the man who called out to him, but he didn't say anything. Instead, he went directly to the other side of the room where he sought out Moe,

Isaac, and Amos.

"Hello, Gentry. Get a drink and join us," Moe suggested.

"No time for that. I've got somethin' I think you fellas are going to want to hear," Roscoe said.

"What's that?" Amos asked.

Gentry shook his head. "Uh-uh. I ain't givin' this away for free."

Lenny was dancing with the daughter of the blacksmith when he saw Moe and the McAfees leave the dance with Deputy Gentry. He didn't know where they were going, but figured it was just as well. When Polly Carpenter had refused to dance with Moe a few minutes ago, his brother had come back over to stand alongside the wall to brood and drink. That was a dangerous combination for Moe, and Lenny had been waiting for the trouble to start.

He was very glad they left, because Lenny especially didn't want any trouble tonight. All he wanted to do tonight was have a good time, and to that end, he had his evening all laid out. He would finish this dance, then go over to the Hermitage for supper. After supper, he planned to wind up over at the Carnation House, where he would spend the night with Lucy.

About five miles out of town, half a dozen men were riding through the darkness, their way lighted by an exceptionally bright moon. Dan Rankin was at the head of the group and when the road crested a hill, he stopped and held up his hand. The others stopped with him.

"There it is, boys," Dan said, pointing to the dark buildings: house, barn, bunkhouse, and granary they lay in a cluster in the little valley below. "The McAfee place."

"Where you think they're a'keepin' our cattle?" Underhill asked.

"Mike said he seen 'em over in the feeder pens," Slim said. "That's the feeder pens, over there behind the barn."

"All right, boys, what do you say we ease on down there, real quiet," Dan said. "Everyone keep together, and keep your eyes open," Dan urged his horse on down the hill and the others followed. One of the horses whinnied, and its rider leaned forward to pat the animal, reassuringly on its neck.

When Moe saw Dan and his men moving like shadows through the sage, he jacked a shell into the chamber of his rifle and waited.

"Do you see 'em?" Isaac McAfee whispered.

"Yeah, I see 'em. They're comin', just like Gentry said they would," Moe said. "Look over there, just this side of that big cottonwood tree," Moe said, pointing.

"Let 'em come. We're ready for 'em," Amos said. He also jacked a round into his rifle.

Moe, Isaac, and Amos had come up with ten dollars apiece to buy the information that Gentry had to sell them. For thirty dollars, Gentry told them that he had learned Dan Rankin and his men were planning a raid on the McAfee Ranch. Moe and the McAfees left the dance immediately and began preparing to meet them. Moe, Isaac, Amos, and eight of the McAfees' most trusted riders were in positions around the feeder pens, hiding behind rocks, buildings, and other convenient places of cover and concealment. Dan Rankin was riding into an ambush.

"There don't seem to be no one around," Slim said. His voice carried well in the darkness, and Moe and the others could hear every word.

"Well, if we're goin' to get our cows back, this has to be the best time for it," Dan said. "I figure the McAfees and most of their outfit has to be in town for the dance."

"Yeah, I'd be there too, if it wasn't for this," Underhill said.

"Which would you rather do, dance or get our cows back?" Levi asked.

"Seein' as how some o' them cows is mine, I reckon I'd rather be here, a-gettin' 'em back," Underhill answered.

As they rode slowly down the hill, they could hear a

gentle lowing from the area of the feeder pens. There they could also see the massed shadows of milling cattle. Their cattle.

"There they are," Dan said, pointing to the feeder pens. "That's about twelve hundred dollars of our money, boys. Let's go get it back."

"Now!" Moe suddenly shouted, his voice cutting through the night like the peal of doom. He stood up, raised his rifle to his shoulder, and fired, and, with a surprised grunt of pain, Levi fell from his saddle.

"What the hell!" Slim shouted. "Where did that come from?"

Frightened and surprised by the sudden and unexpected ambush, Rankin's men tried to control their bolting horses.

"They were waitin' on us!" Dan shouted, managing to snap off a shot toward the flashes of rifles and pistols that were now shooting at him. "Get out of here, boys!" Out of the corner of his eye he saw another of his men going down.

"Boss, they got Levi and Underhill!" Slim shouted. Getting his horse under control, he jerked it around and dug his spurs into the animal's flanks. Just as he did so, a bullet crashed into the back of Slim's head.

"Slim!" Dan shouted, but his next word was cut off as a bullet entered his own back, tore through his heart, then exited through his chest.

For no more than half a minute, the night was lit with the muzzle flashes of those who had waited in ambush. The guns roared and bullets whined, then, as suddenly as it had begun, the firefight was over. Now the final gunshot was rolling back as an echo as Moe, Isaac, Amos, and the others stood up, cautiously. Not one of the approaching riders was still horsed. Not one of the ambushers had been hit.

Holding smoking guns at the ready, Moe and the McAfees walked slowly through the dark to look through the twisted forms lying on the ground. None were moving and all were silent. Amos was the first one to them, and he began poking at them with the toe of his boot.

"Any of 'em alive?" Isaac called.

Amos looked back at his brother and shook his head. "Don't think so. Ain't none of 'em breathin'."

"Whooee!" Moe shouted. "We got 'em! We got ever' damn one of 'em!"

"What do we do with 'em now?" Isaac asked.

"Sometime before mornin' we'll load 'em in a wagon and take 'em into town," Moe suggested.

"And do what with 'em?"

"We'll just leave 'em there."

"When the townspeople wake up and find 'em there, that's goin' to cause quite a stink," Amos said. Then, realizing the double entendre of his comment, he laughed. "Hey, you fellas get that? These here dead bodies is goin' to cause a stink?" He laughed again.

"You think it's a good idea to take 'em into town?" Isaac asked.

"Why not? We got nothin' to hide. They the ones come out here to attack us. We didn't go after them. The deputy can vouch for that."

"Moe's right," Amos said. "We got nothin' to hide. And the way I look at it, this'll be a pretty good sign for anyone else that takes a notion to steal any of our cattle."

"Yeah," Moe said. "Or even for somebody who might decide to steal back any of the cattle we already stole."

The three men laughed again and the McAfee hands, who were still up by the feeder pens, were struck by the macabre scene of their employers laughing loudly while poking through the bodies of six dead men.

Chapter Twelve

No one in Shafter knew about the short, fierce battle that had just taken place out at the McAfee Ranch. Here, the laughter and the friendly exchange of conversation continued as the partygoers left the hotel to start back home ... townspeople, miners, and ranchers alike. The members of the Shafter Spring Square Dance Committee were congratulating each other on the success of the event, not only for its social significance, but also because it seemed to draw the townspeople, miners, and ranchers closer together.

They weren't entirely blind to the fact that the Tuckers and the McAfees had left the party early, thus eliminating the biggest potential source of trouble. Still, they told each other, it had been a successful experiment, and should be tried again.

Will offered to walk Polly back to the Carnation

House and she accepted. Then, with goodbyes, good natured shouts, and laughter still ringing in their ears, they started down the street.

"I had a wonderful time tonight, Will," Polly said. She put her arm through his.

"I did too," Will replied.

"I just wish the rest of Marie's girls could have gone."

"It wouldn't have bothered me any," Will said. "Hell, I don't think it would've bothered anyone except a few of the old crones who don't have anything better to do."

"I know," Polly said. She sighed. "And, sad to say, I was once one of those old crones."

Will laughed.

"What is it?"

"Well, you're not old, and you are anything but a crone," he said.

"Maybe not, but I must confess that my social mores have changed considerably since coming out West. I have seen, and done, and accepted things that I never would have done before. I mean, here I am, letting a man I've only known for a short time, walk me back to my room in a bawdy house." Polly laughed. "Who knows what I am liable to do next?"

"Yeah," Will said, smiling at her. "Who knows?"

At that moment they heard boots clumping on the wooden sidewalk as someone was chasing after them.

Turning toward the sound, Will saw that it was one of the men he played poker with on a regular basis, a man who worked as a freight wagon driver for the Mina Grande.

"Marshal Crockett, you'd better come quick!"

"What is it, Tim?"

"That Mex fella, the one that works over to the whorehouse? He's in trouble. I'm afraid he's goin' to be killed."

"What?" Polly asked in alarm. "Will, is he talking about Señor Munoz?"

"Munoz, yeah, that's the one," Tim said. "Some drunk cowboy is givin' him a hard time."

"We've got to help him," Polly said, starting toward the Dust Cutter.

"Not we ... me. You go on home," Will ordered. "I'll take care of it."

The Dust Cutter was strangely quiet when Will stepped through the door. The piano music, the card playing, and even the conversation had all stopped. Everyone in the saloon had moved to one side of the room or the other, while in the middle stood the Mexican cook from the Carnation House. Munoz had an expression of terror on his face, brought on by the fact that a cowboy was pointing a gun at him.

Will recognized the cowboy as a man named Townsend. Townsend had never given him any trouble before, but he was obviously looking for trouble now.

"Munoz, what is it? What's going on?" Will asked.

"Ask the gringo," Munoz answered. "I think maybe he wants to kill me."

"Townsend, what are you doing with that gun?" Will asked. "You know we put a ban on against carrying guns tonight because of the dance."

"I didn't have it when I was at the dance."

"The ban was for all night, whether you were at the dance or not."

"That's a mighty dumb idea if you ask me," Townsend said.

"Well, that's the point, Townsend. I don't recall asking you about it when I came up with the plan," Will said. He looked around the saloon. "Anyone else in here armed?"

"Nobody else is heeled, Marshal," Henry, the bartender, said. "Ever'one is clean as a whistle."

Will looked back at Townsend, then held out his hand. "Then that means you're the only one here carrying a gun, and you're the only one here causing trouble. Why don't you give it to me?"

Townsend shook his head. "Uh-uh. Not until I kill this here Mexican."

"You planning on killing him in cold blood?"

"Yep."

"Well, then let me shake your hand," Will said.

Still grinning, drunkenly, Townsend switched his gun from his right hand to his left, then extended his hand. In a quick, abrupt maneuver, Will managed to snatch the gun from Townsend with his left hand while at the same time clipping him hard on the chin with his right. Townsend went down and out.

"You got that bucket of mop water behind the bar?" Will asked the bartender.

"Yeah, I got it."

"Hand it to me."

Henry bent down, picked up the bucket and gave it to Will. Will poured it on Townsend, who sat up, coughing and spitting dirty water.

"Munoz, get on back to the Carnation House," Will said.

"Si, Señor. Gracias."

"Hey, you're lettin' him go!" Townsend complained.

"Yeah? Well, I can't be bothered with that," Will said. "Come on. I'm throwin' your ass in jail, but I'm not carryin' you down there. You're goin' to have to walk."

Defiantly, Townsend put his wet hat back on. "What if I tell you I ain't goin' to walk?"

"I'll shoot you in the foot."

"No you won't. You're wearin' a badge."

"Don't let the badge fool you. I'm not like any lawman you ever knew."

"Is that a fact? Well, I'm sittin' right here, 'cause I'm

bettin' you won't shoot me in the foot," Townsend said with a snide smile. Pulling his knees up in front of him, he wrapped his arms around his legs and glared defiantly at Will.

Suddenly, and unexpectedly, there was the loud explosion of a gunshot. When the billowing smoke drifted away, the surprised patrons saw Will standing there, holding a smoking pistol. Will had shot at Townsend's foot, clipping the edge of the boot sole. The bullet also creased Townsend's little toe and he grabbed it, howling with pain.

"I guess you lose the bet," Will said. "Now, get up while you can still walk, or I'll fix it so you really do have to be carried. Either way, you're going to spend the night in jail."

"No, no," Townsend said. "Don't shoot again. I'm goin', I'm goin'." He hopped up as quickly as he could under the circumstances, then, limping, started toward the jail, followed by the laughter of all who were in the saloon.

"I'm here to collect the tax," Gentry said.

Marie shook her head. "I paid Sheriff Jones the tax last week. Don't you two ever talk?"

"Uh-uh," Gentry said with an evil grin. "This is a new, special tax that was just put on."

"I don't know anything about any special tax."

"Like I said, it's one that was just put on." Gentry cackled. "Fact is, I just put it on myself. It's twenty dollars."

"I'm not about to pay you twenty dollars, Deputy," Marie insisted.

"Well, there's a way you can avoid paying the tax. I'm sure me 'n you can work something out, if you know what I mean."

"No, I don't know what you mean."

"Sure, you do. All you have to do is go upstairs with me."

"Deputy, you know I don't do that. Go down and find a woman in one of the cribs."

"I don't want one of them, I want you," Gentry said in a coarse and demanding tone. He reached out to put his hand on her shoulder. "And the way I see it, there's nothin' you can do to stop me."

"I'm not so sure about that," Marie said.

"What ... what's that? Gentry asked as he felt something sharp poking into his stomach.

"This is a hunting knife with a forged blade honed to an edge sharp enough to cut paper. I think I can stop you."

Gentry backed away, holding his hands up.

"Hold on there, now. You just hold on," Gentry said.

At that moment Gid was coming down the stairs with Lucy. Lucy was laughing at something Gid had just said.

"Oh, oh."

"What is it, Lucy? What's wrong?"

"*He's* wrong," Lucy said, pointing toward Gentry.

"Excuse me for a moment," Gid said.

Gid walked over to where Gentry and Marie were standing, and he saw Marie with a knife in her hand. She was holding it like someone who knew how to use it—low and lying sideways in the palm of her hand.

"Well, I was going to take a hand, but it would appear that you have everything under control," Gid said.

"I believe I do."

"Miss Lacoste, Lucy and I were just wondering if you'd like to come into the parlor and have a glass of wine with us. That is, if you aren't too busy."

"Oh, I believe Mr. Gentry and I have concluded our business," Marie said. She smiled at Gid. "I would love to have a drink with you and Lucy."

"You had no right to pull that knife on me," Gentry said. "Have you forgotten? I'm the deputy sheriff."

"And I'm a deputy town marshal and as it so happens right now, you're in my town," Gid said.

Gentry stared at Gid with impotent rage, and then he turned and walked away. Not until Gentry left the house did the others who had witnessed the interplay applaud.

"That's some knife you've got there," Gid said.

"Would you like to see it?" Marie invited, handing it to him.

The blade was polished steel and the handle was made

of stag horn, into which a horse's head had been carved.

"This was given to me some time ago by someone who called himself an admirer."

"It's quite a gift."

"Well, he was what you might call a unique admirer. You may have heard of him; he was a general in the Confederate army. Nathan Bedford Forrest."

Gid smiled. "Oh yeah, I've heard of him."

———————

Polly was just coming up the front steps as Gentry was leaving.

"Good evening, Deputy," she said, pleasantly.

"Get the hell out of my way, whore," Gentry said as he passed by.

"Yes, well you have a pleasant night now, you hear?" Polly said, putting as much sweetness into her comment as she could.

"*Arrumph*," Gentry replied, though it was more of a growl.

Polly couldn't help but smile. She had learned long ago that a 'too sweet' response to rudeness could be more effective than the most biting riposte.

Chapter Thirteen

When Polly returned home to the Carnation House, she was met in the parlor by half a dozen of the girls.

"She's back!"

"Tell us all about it!"

"Yes, do tell. Was the music just wonderful? We could hear it, even down here!"

They were as excited as schoolgirls as they crowded around Polly to listen to her report of the biggest social event in Shafter's history.

"Well?" one of the girls asked, impatiently.

"Well, what?" Polly replied.

"Are you going to tell us about the dance? Or, are you going to make us wait until Lucy and the others come down?" Daisy asked.

"We won't see Lucy again tonight," Cathleen said with a knowing smile. "Lenny Tucker is here."

"That's all right, I'm not going to make you wait," Polly replied with a little laugh. "I'll tell you everything I can. And if I have to begin again when someone new comes, then what is the harm? But, where do I start? What do you want to know?"

"What did everyone wear?" someone asked.

"Yes, were the dresses beautiful?"

"Did the women wear jewelry?"

"Were there good things to eat?"

"Was the music as good as it sounded?"

Polly laughed. "Wait a minute, hold it, one question at a time, please," she said. "Just be patient, I'll tell you everything, I promise."

For the next several minutes Polly did all she could do to make the party happen for them. And whenever one of the girls who had been absent when she started talking drifted into the parlor, she would start over. There was never the slightest complaint from those who had already heard the first part of the story about having to listen again.

Polly's audiences seemed insatiable, and she described the dresses she saw, even though she had no idea who was wearing them, and the decorations, and the band, and the food, until finally the subject was exhausted and she said she could think of nothing more to tell them.

"All right, but tomorrow, when you've had time to

think about it some, you must tell it all over again," one of the girls insisted.

"Yes, and also tomorrow, tell us which dress you think was most beautiful."

"I promise," Polly said. "But I have to go upstairs and get some sleep now. It's been a very long and tiring day for me."

"Polly," one of the girls said as Polly started out of the parlor. Polly turned and looked back toward her. "We're really glad you went to the party," the girl said. "Thank you for going, and for sharing it with us."

Polly nodded, feeling a twinge of guilt that she had been able to enjoy the evening while the closest the girls could come was listening to her description of the event. Seeing how important this little contact with the rest of the world was to them, Polly made a private vow that she would give it even more thought tonight. That way, when she renewed her conversation with them again tomorrow, she would be able to make it even more exciting.

She left the parlor and went out into the hallway to the foot of the stairs. Looking toward the kitchen, she happened to see Doc Hawkins talking to Señor Munoz, and it wasn't until that moment that she remembered Will had gone over to the Dust Cutter to rescue Munoz from a drunken cowboy. Obviously, the rescue had been effective, for Munoz was here.

"Oh, Señor Munoz, thank goodness you aren't hurt," Polly said, going to him, feeling guilty because she hadn't even thought about him until this moment. "I heard that some drunken cowboy had accosted you.

"*Si, Señorita*, he did. But I am pleased to say that Marshal Crockett put the bad man in jail."

"Good for the marshal. Jail is exactly where such a ruffian should be. And good evening, to you, Doc," Polly added. "I didn't mean to overlook you; it's just that I was worried about Señor Munoz's safety."

"Quite all right," Doc said. "I heard you talking with the other young ladies in the parlor about the square dance. I am glad you had a good time."

"Yes, thank you. I did have a good time. I wish you had come, Doc. Had you been there, we could have shared a dance."

"Yes, my absence was my misfortune, Miss Carpenter," Doc said.

"Perhaps some other time?" Polly said.

"It would be a privilege and an honor," Doc said.

With a parting nod to the two men, she started back toward the stairs. That was when she saw Gid coming toward the kitchen.

"Señor Munoz, I'm so hungry I could eat a mule. You got anything in the kitchen I could eat?" Gid called toward the kitchen.

Munoz chuckled. "I do not have a mule, *Señor.* But for you, I can always find something," he answered.

Gid tossed a casual greeting toward Polly, then he headed for the kitchen. Marie came over to speak with Polly.

"It was good of you to share your observations with the other girls," Marie said, as the two ascended the stairs together.

"Oh, I enjoyed sharing with them, but I feel so guilty that they weren't able to enjoy the party as well."

"Don't feel guilty, dear. They did enjoy the party, through you."

"Marie, why do you suppose Doc didn't go to the dance?" she asked. "Do the townspeople have the same disdain for him that they have for the girls who work here?"

Marie laughed. "Are you asking if the town has disdain for Doc? Honey, it's more likely that Doc has disdain for the town."

"I can believe that about Doc and this town," Polly said. "But, what about women? Does Doc have disdain for women as well? I've never seen him with any of the girls who work here. Have you?"

Marie looked puzzled, as if she, too, had been contemplating the question. "You know, I've wondered about that too," she admitted. "Doc was always one of our regulars, but something happened to him the last time he went to El Paso and it changed him. He doesn't go upstairs with any of the girls anymore."

"What happened?" Polly asked.

"I don't have any idea what it might be."

"And when he came back from El Paso acting differently, you didn't ask him what was wrong?"

"Honey, Doc isn't the kind of man you ask what is wrong. If something is wrong and he wants you to know, he'll tell you. Otherwise it's best to keep your questions to yourself."

"Yes, I can understand that. Doc is such a ... private person."

At that moment Polly heard someone playing the piano downstairs. The music was beautiful, filling the house with rich, full chords. A lilting melody seemed to weave through the piece like a thread of gold woven into a very fine cloth.

"Oh, my!" Polly gasped. She held her hand up. "Listen to that beautiful music!"

She couldn't believe what she was hearing. She had attended concerts of the finest pianists in the country, and yet she could honestly say that what she was listening to now was as beautiful as any piano concerto she had ever heard.

"Why, that's Mozart," she said in surprise. "That is *Sonata in F major.* Who on earth would have thought that there would be anyone in Shafter with the musical skills to play so beautifully?"

"Don't you know who that is? Marie asked.

Polly shook her head. "I haven't the slightest idea," she answered.

"It's Doc Hawkins," Marie said.

"*That* is Doc Hawkins? I'm amazed. Marie, that's the playing of an accomplished musician."

"Doc is a skilled musician. Go and see for yourself, if you don't believe me," Marie said.

Polly walked back to the head of the stairs so she could look down into the parlor. She saw Doc sitting at the piano, leaning toward the keyboard with his head tilted slightly as he played. The girls who had earlier gathered so eagerly around Polly to hear her stories were now sitting about the parlor, on the sofa, on chairs, and even on the floor, listening in rapt silence to the music that was spilling out of the battered old piano in the parlor.

Polly stood at the head of the stairs, letting the music sweep over her. Never had she heard anything more beautiful ... it was agony and ecstasy, and it stirred her very soul. She saw, too, that the girls in the parlor were equally moved, for they were wiping their eyes, and even Marie shed a tear or two.

Was it possible? Polly wondered. Could this be the same man who could call down three armed men and set them running just from fear of his name? What personal and private hell had this man been through to bring him to a place like Shafter? He could be filling concert halls in New York, Boston, Philadelphia, and even London and Paris if he wanted to. Instead, he was sitting in the parlor of a whorehouse in a town so small that its entire population could fit into one of the larger concert halls.

Finally, the piece ended and Doc poured himself a glass of whiskey, then played another song, this one light and bouncy, and more in keeping with the type of music one might expect in such a place.

With that, the mood was broken, and after telling Marie good night, Polly let herself into her room, where she went to bed.

As she lay in bed watching moon shadows play upon the wall, she thought of her position here. Her mother had been the grand dame of Memphis society, and she insisted that Polly belong to all the 'right' clubs and organizations for proper women. And yet here she was, living in a house of prostitution.

She knew that Marie wanted all the girls to regard each other as family and though Polly did not share 'the profession' with them, she had never had more dear friends. They were, indeed, her sisters.

Chapter Fourteen

On the road leading into Shafter from the McAfee Ranch, Isaac McAfee was riding one horse and leading another. Amos McAfee was riding alongside him. They were both accompanying a wagon being driven by Moe Tucker and pulled by a team of mules. The wagon was being taken into town. There, the three men planned to disconnect the team and take it back, leaving the wagon and its macabre load parked on Main Street in the middle of Shafter.

Always an early riser, Gid walked through the predawn darkness toward the town marshal's office, where he planned to put on a pot of coffee. He was already hungry, but the coffee would have to hold him until the Hermitage opened for breakfast.

He saw a wagon ahead and at first thought it was sitting in front of the apothecary next door. When he got a little closer, though, he realized that the wagon was actually parked in front of the marshal's office, a situation he found curious. The fact that there was no team attached to the wagon made the situation even more curious, so he quickened his pace to see what it was about.

When he reached the wagon, he saw that it wasn't empty. There was something in the back, covered by a tarpaulin. Gid grabbed a corner of the tarpaulin and pulled it to one side.

"Son of a bitch!" he said aloud.

There were six men in the wagon. All six were riddled with bullets ... and all six were dead. One of the six was Dan Rankin.

When J.C. Malone went down to the hardware store where the bodies had been taken, he had them strapped to one-by-six planks and propped up against the front of the store so he could take their pictures. The sight of so many bodies in one place drew a rather sizeable crowd and they stood around in curiosity, watching Malone work.

Malone, ever the good newspaper man, got the pictures, which he would display in the front window of the newspaper office, as well as the story.

BLOODY RANGE BATTLE
Fight Over Stolen Cattle
Six Are Killed

On the 5th, while most citizens of the city and county were enjoying a wonderful dance party sponsored by the Shafter Square Dance Committee, the Grim Reaper wrought a terrible carnage out on the range.

Rancher Dan Rankin, convinced that his cattle had been stolen by the Tuckers and the McAfees, and unable to find satisfaction from the county sheriff's department, did what any self-respecting man would do. He took matters into his own hands. Leading a party of his own men to the McAfee Ranch, Rankin was bent upon recovering his stolen cattle. The visit was made in the middle of the night, with the intent of using the cover of darkness.

To the great misfortune and ultimate doom of Dan Rankin and those brave lads who rode with him, however, the McAfees were warned by Deputy Sheriff Roscoe Gentry of their approach. With neighbor Moe Tucker and no fewer than eight armed men, the McAfees waited until the riders were in their midst.

At this point there is some confusion as to what happened. Moe Tucker says that a warning was called out to the would-be cattle-thieves, and they were given the opportunity to throw down their arms and return to their own ranch, empty-handed. Other sources have insisted to this newspaper, however, that no such warning was given. Instead, the defenders opened fire from their position in ambuscade, sending deadly missiles of death through the darkness.

It was not a battle as much as it was a slaughter, and the results were, predictably, very lopsided. For those who waited in ambush at the McAfee Ranch—Moe Tucker, Isaac and Amos McAfee, and the armed men who were at their side—not one wound was sustained. But for Dan Rankin and the brave young men who rode with him on that fateful night, it was their last moment on earth, as all were killed.

Two days after Dan, Slim, Underhill and the others were buried, Moe Tucker hired a lawyer from El Paso to file a claim in circuit court against Dan's ranch. Lenny was uncomfortable with the claim and told Moe as much, but when the claim was presented, it included Lenny as one of the plaintiffs.

"Hilda Tucker's will plainly stated that Dan Rankin must operate the ranch for ten years," Moe's lawyer said in his presentation to the judge. "He clearly did not do so, thus the land and all property, fixed and moveable, must return to Moe and Lenny Tucker."

There were many in the town who thought it seemed unfair, pointing out that Dan didn't operate the ranch for ten years because Moe killed him before the ten years was up.

However, it was also pointed out that Dan's death had already been ruled as a justifiable homicide. And, while there were several who didn't like Moe Tucker and wanted to see him fail in his lawsuit, there was really no one to argue the case against him, since Dan Rankin had left no known survivors. Thus, regardless of how unpopular his decision might be, the judge had no choice but to rule in favor of Moe and Lenny Tucker. The Rankin land, and all property, fixed and moveable, was awarded to Moe and Lenny Tucker.

The piano in the Dust Cutter was playing merrily, but the noise in the saloon was such that no one could hear it from more than ten feet away. In one corner Moe, Isaac, and Amos, and a few cowboys, including Asa Townsend, were singing in competition with the piano. They had been drinking and singing in celebration of the judge's order ever since the order was handed down.

When Doc came into the saloon after supper, he saw that it was much too noisy for any kind of a serious card game, so he stepped up to the bar.

"Hello, Doc," the bartender asked. "Your usual?"

"Yes, thanks, Henry," Doc replied.

Henry pulled a bottle of aged bourbon from beneath the bar. It was a brand that he kept on hand especially for Doc and kept under the bar just for him. He poured Doc a drink, put the bottle back under the bar, then returned to rubbing his rag on the bar. If anyone had asked Henry, he would have told them he was cleaning the bar. In reality he was just spreading the spilled liquor around, which did nothing toward improving the bar surface. The bar still reflected the scars inflicted upon it by the shotgun blast of Ernest Fowler when he tried to kill Will Crockett on the first day Will and Gid arrived.

Doc turned his back to the bar to look out over the raucous celebration.

"How long have they been at it?" he asked.

"Ever since they come out of court this afternoon," Henry said. "Don't know why the McAfees are celebratin' so. Moe Tucker is the only one who gained by it. Well, Moe and Lenny."

"Has Lenny been in here?"

"No," Henry answered. "If you ask me, he's a little shamed by the whole thing."

"Hey! Hey!" Moe shouted to the others, after taking another long pull on a bottle of whiskey. "Are we just goin' to sit around here suckin' on a bottle like a baby on a tit, or are we all goin' over to the Carnation House?"

"Now, Moe, you know we ain't welcome at the Carnation House," Amos said, shaking his finger back and forth. "The McAfees and the Tuckers just ain't welcome there."

"That ain't true," Isaac said. "Us McAfees ain't welcome, 'n ole' Moe here ain't welcome. But little Lenny boy? Why, he's welcome as rain. Why is that, Moe? Why is Lenny welcome and you ain't?"

"'Cause Lenny's got good manners," Moe said. "He's my little brother and I raised him up proper."

"Too bad you didn't learn some of them manners yourself. If you had some of 'em, maybe we wouldn't get turned away ever' time we tried to get into that fancy whorehouse."

"We'll get in there tonight," Moe said.

"Yeah? What makes you think so?"

"'Cause I'm celebratin', and I don't intend to get turned away tonight," Moe answered. "And if you're men, you'll go with me. All of you," he said, taking in the handful of cowboys who had been a part of the celebration all day.

"Sure, why not?" Isaac said. "Hell, I'll go with you." He stood up, drained the last of the bottle and tossed it over his head casually. It hit the corner of the bar, then smashed into little pieces, but the three men didn't even look around at it as they stepped outside.

"They's goin' to be a shootin' for sure," someone said. "I seen both the Crocketts down there a while ago."

"Come on, let's go watch!" another said, and a moment later there was a mad rush for the doors.

"Doc, you'd better ..." Henry started, then stopped when he saw that Doc was no longer standing at the bar.

Word had preceded the crowd, so that by the time Moe and those with him reached Carnation House, Will and Gid were already standing out on the front porch. They stood there like unmovable statues as the crowd arrived from the saloon, then arrayed itself in a half circle around the front.

Moe Tucker, Isaac and Amos McAfee, and the three cowboys who had been with them were standing in the dirt of the street, looking up. The only light came from a kerosene lamp that gleamed from the wall right behind the Crocketts. It cast a golden bubble of light that splashed out into the street, making deep shadows on the faces of everyone present.

"I believe you gentlemen have come to a place where you are not wanted," Will said, speaking in a low, quiet voice, all the more menacing because of its apparent lack of emotion.

"Get out of the way, Crockett," Moe called. "Me 'n my friends is comin' in." In contrast, Moe's voice was loud and threatening. "You got that, Will Crockett? We're comin' in."

"No, I don't think so, Tucker," Will answered as calmly as before.

"What makes you think we ain't?"

"Because we won't let you," Will replied.

"Yeah? Well the only way you gonna stop us is to shoot us," Moe said. "And there's six of us and only two of you."

"Make that three," another voice said. Doc Hawkins appeared from the dark, then stepped up onto the porch and turned to face the crowd.

"All right, so there are three of you. We still outnumber you two to one," Moe blustered. "You really want to fight it out with us?"

"Yes, I do," Will said. "I'm ready to settle the issue right here and right now." He dropped his arm loosely to his side. One of the three cowboys who had come with Moe and the McAfees was Asa Townsend. "Townsend, are you dealing yourself into this hand?"

All conversation halted then, and there was a collective holding of breath as the crowd waited for the play to unfold.

"No," Townsend suddenly said. "No, I was just out to have a little fun, that's all. I ... I don't want no part of this." He put his hands up in the air. "Marshal, when the shooting starts I ain't goin' to be a part of it," he added, backing away slowly.

"Me neither," one of the others said, and, cautiously, two cowboys joined the first.

"Well, Tucker, what do you say?" Will baited. "Are we going to do this or not?"

"What's goin' on down here?" another voice asked.

"You folks break it up. Break it up and go on home," the voice said authoritatively.

The voice belonged to Sheriff Jones who moved through the crowd, shoving people roughly to one side or the other.

"All right, all right, Sheriff," Moe suddenly said, holding his hands out in front of him to show that he was not about to make a hostile move. "We ain't goin' to draw. Put your hands out, boys," he said to the others. "If anything happens sheriff, it's the Crocketts'doin's. We ain't goin' to draw."

"Go on home now, boys, the show is over," Jones said to the gathered crowd when Moe and the McAfees had walked away without unsheathing their weapons.

"What the hell did you butt in for?" Will asked as the crowd began disappearing into the darkness.

"Hell, somebody had to take a hand," Jones said. "Things was startin' to get out of control."

"Yeah, well, I was about to put things back into control," Will said.

"How did you plan to do that?"

"I was going to kill them," Will answered unequivocally.

Chapter Fifteen

When Will, Gid, and Doc went back inside, Marie thanked them for turning Moe Tucker and the McAfees away.

"Why couldn't Moe Tucker be more like his brother?" she asked. "Lenny is upstairs right now with Lucy. He is such a well-behaved young man. And Moe and the McAfees do nothing but make trouble."

"What kind of trouble?" Will asked.

"Just … trouble," Marie said, hesitantly.

"Have any of them ever hit any of the girls?" Will asked.

"A couple of times. That's why I won't let them in."

"Miss Lacoste, would you mind if I played the piano for a few minutes?" Doc Hawkins

"No, of course not. The girls and I, even the customers, love to hear you play."

"And I love to play for you," Doc said.

Doc walked into the parlor and sat down. As he began

to play, Doc felt himself slipping away from the parlor of a whorehouse in a small western town; instead he was at another time and another place.

Fifteen hundred people filled the Crystal Palace in London, England to hear the latest musical sensation from America. When the curtain opened, the audience applauded as John Hawkins walked out onto the stage, flipped the tails back from his swallowtail coat then took his seat at the piano.

The auditorium grew quiet and John began to play Beethoven's Concerto Number Five in E Flat Major. The music filled the concert hall and caressed the collective soul of the audience.

Doc may have been imagining fifteen hundred people, but in reality, there were only ten in the parlor: Will, Gid, Marie, Lenny, Lucy, Daisy, Cathleen, Wanda, Doc, and Polly. And, like Doc, Polly's own imagination had put her in a concert hall in St. Louis sitting between her mother and father and listening to ... she just now realized with a start, *this same man.*

It was something magical. Doc Hawkins, who she now knew was John Hawkins, managed with his playing, to resurrect the genius of the composer so that Polly was listening to John Hawkins and Ludwig Beethoven as if they were one and the same.

After he finished the piece the applause was as genuine and even more heartfelt from his small audience as it had been anywhere he had ever played. Doc stood and, unself-consciously bowed. As the others began to move about, Polly walked to him and put her hand on his shoulder. Her eyes were brimmed with tears.

"I heard you perform at The Varieties Theater in St. Louis," she said.

"No, I'm sure you must be mistaken."

"You played this piece, as well as Beethoven's Concerto Number Five, Beethoven's Moonlight Sonata, Chopin's Nocturne in E Flat, *and* Liszt – La Campanella."

Doc closed his eyes, bowed his head, and pinched the bridge of his nose. He was quiet for a long moment before he replied.

"You have an excellent memory, my dear," he said.

"It was you, wasn't it?" she asked, her voice rising in excitement.

"Yes, it was I."

"I don't understand. What happened? Why are you here, in this place like ..." Polly halted in mid-sentence, realizing that this line of conversation was painful for Doc.

"I ... I'm sorry, Doc. I have no right to ask such questions."

"You have every right to ask, just as I have every right to refuse to answer," Doc replied.

"Doctor Hawkins, regardless of whatever personal hell you have gone through, you have brought beauty to the world, just as you brought beauty here, tonight," Polly said, "and I thank you for that."

Doc Hawkins lifted Polly's hand to his lips and kissed it. For that moment in time, he wasn't a consumptive alcoholic gunman, and she wasn't a clerk in a bordello. He was a gentleman and she was a lady, and this was the Court of St. James.

The mood was broken when Gid came up to join them. "If I could play as well as Doc, would you let me kiss your hand?"

Smiling, Polly lifted her hand to his lips and Gid kissed it.

Polly turned and joined the others who had enjoyed the impromptu concert.

"That Doc sure is a good piano player," Lucy said.

"No he isn't," Polly said.

"What? What do mean? Didn't you just hear him?"

"He isn't a piano player, he's a pianist."

"Yes, I would agree with that," Lenny said. "He's much more than a piano player."

"Lenny, why don't you join Will and me for a drink at the Dust Cutter?" Gid asked.

"All right," Lenny agreed.

"And I think it's time I had a stiff drink, as well," Doc said as he rose from the piano.

"Wait, Lenny, if you go you will come back," Lucy said.

Lenny looked at Marie. "I'm a Tucker. Am I welcomed here?"

Marie laughed. "Of course you are! You're one of our most welcomed visitors, isn't that right, Lucy?"

Lucy didn't answer. She just smiled.

A few minutes later the four men were sitting at a table in the Dust Cutter. Will, Gid, and Lenny were drinking beer, and Doc was on his second whiskey.

"Lucy told me that you turned my brother away from Carnation House," Lenny said.

"We did," Will replied. "But Moe and the others left with no trouble."

"I'm glad there was no trouble. My brother can be a ... difficult man sometimes."

Gid chucked. "What do you mean when you say sometimes? Hell, the son of a bitch has been difficult every time I've ever seen him."

"He is my brother," Lenny said pointedly.

"I'm sorry," Gid said. "Yes, he is that. But what I'm wondering is how did it happen?"

"How did what happen?"

"I think what my brother is trying to say is, how did you turn out the way you are, and how did your brother turn out the way he is?"

"I don't know that I can answer that. I do know that Moe has always believed that he has to prove himself. At first it was to Pop, but Pop has been dead for three years, so I don't know who he's trying to prove himself to, now. As for me, well I've always tried to be sort of easy-going and casual, I guess."

Doc lifted his glass. "Here is to the easy-going, casual, insouciant Lenny. In a way that's difficult to explain, you and I, Lenny my good man, are kindred spirits."

"Friends across the lines," Will said as he lifted his beer mug. Gid and Lenny did as well, and the four glasses clinked across the middle of the table.

Back at Carnation House, all the girls were occupied either with a visitor in their rooms or preparing themselves for the evening. Marie and Polly were in a small private anteroom that was used as an office.

"Doc Hawkins is such a strange man," Polly said. "He has the talent to make the world more beautiful with his music, and yet he is ..." she paused trying to find a way to end her sentence then simply added, "here."

"I have seen men like him before," Marie said, "Men who saw terrible things in the war and who have not been able to recover from it.

"And Doc is a special case. He was raised in wealth, his whole life was beauty and luxury, and for such a person, the horrors of war have an even more terrible effect. Then he came back to find that the world he had always known was gone.

"Doc has put a shell around himself, my dear. From time to time he will open that shell just a bit and expose himself as he did tonight with his music. And that leaves him very vulnerable."

"I saw a little of that a few minutes ago," Polly said.

"I think you've been good for his wounded soul," Marie said. She smiled, then took Polly's hand in hers. "As a matter of fact you've been good for all of us."

Polly smiled. "The girls did seem to enjoy it when I started describing the dance to them, didn't they?"

"We all did, but that's not the only thing I'm talking about. You aren't one of us, Polly, and yet, you are. You don't see us as prostitutes or soiled doves or whatever word people use for our kind. You see us as friends."

Polly shook her head. "No, I don't see you as friends at all." Then when she saw the disturbed look on Marie's face, she smiled. "I see you as my sisters."

Marie jumped from her chair and embraced Polly. The two women were acutely aware of their unique relationship.

As Marie lay in bed that night, she realized more than ever, that the visit she had made to her lawyer a few days earlier had been the right thing to do. Finally, with Doc Hawkins' music still playing in her mind, she drifted off to sleep.

She had no idea how long she had been asleep when she felt a hand clasping across her mouth preventing her from crying out.

"You just lay there 'n be quiet, 'n this'll all be over in a few minutes," a man's gruff voice said.

Marie turned her head so that she got her mouth free. "Who are you?" she asked, her voice thickened by fright. "What do you want?"

"This is where you come to get a woman, ain't it? That's why I'm here."

"Not this way," Marie said.

Her assailant responded with a low, growling chuckle. "You ain't got much to say about it."

All the while Marie was keeping him talking, her hand was searching on her bed until she found it. Wrapping her fingers around the handle of her staghorn knife, she brought it up in an attempt to stab her attacker, but he saw the movement and was able to grab her wrist.

"Huh uh, that's not going to work this time, girly."

As she struggled with him, she felt a sharp pain draw across her neck, then dizziness, then nothing.

Chapter Sixteen

Will and Gid were having breakfast when Rupert Jackson came into the Hermitage. As a member of the town council, a visit from Jackson didn't seem all that unusual to them. But this morning Jackson was wearing his high hat and a dark jacket with tails—his undertaking garb.

"What is it, Jackson?" Will asked. "Why the get-up?"

Jackson looked at the brothers with an expression of practiced solemnity.

"I'm afraid I have some bad news," he said. "I'm afraid it is Miss Marie Lacoste herself."

"What?" Gid asked, standing up so quickly that his chair fell over. Everyone else in the restaurant looked over at him in curiosity. "Are you telling me Marie is dead?"

The words buzzed around the restaurant as it was passed from table to table.

"Theresa found her this morning," Jackson said. "She was in her own bed, with her throat cut."

"Son of a bitch!" Gid said. He shook his head. "Son of a bitch! Who could do such a thing?"

By the time Will and Gid reached the Carnation House, a crowd of solemn onlookers had gathered around outside. They stood on the side of the street, on the lawn, along the edges of the flower beds, and up on the front porch, but none of them had gone inside. They parted to let Will and Gid in.

Inside, all the girls were gathered in the parlor, and all were crying. Polly, seeing Will and Gid, came over to them. She went into Will's arms and cried into his chest. Lucy came to Gid.

"Did anyone hear anything, or see anything?" Gid asked.

"Not a sight, not a sound," Lucy answered. "We've already talked among ourselves, and we don't have any idea who it was."

"Will, do you think there is a chance you can find out who did this terrible thing?" Polly asked.

"I don't know," Will admitted. "There is always a chance, but, like I've told you before, my brother and I aren't really lawmen."

"You will try, though?"

"Yes, of course we will try."

"I had no idea how much I would miss her," Polly said. "She was my ... my anchor, out here."

One of those most devastated by Marie's death was the maid, Theresa. She was standing over in a corner, alone, sobbing out loud.

"Look at poor Theresa," Polly said. "She seems to be taking it harder than any of us."

Polly and Will walked over to comfort Theresa.

"Theresa, are you all right?" Polly asked.

"Oh, Señorita Carpenter," Theresa said. "Señorita Lacoste was such a good woman. I know she was a sinner, but she was a good woman. I have said many times the Rosary, and I have prayed that God will not send her to hell. Do you think He will?"

"If you were God, would you send her to hell?" Polly asked.

Theresa crossed herself quickly. "No," she said.

"Why not?"

"Because I know her. She was a soiled dove, yes, but she was a good woman. I know her."

"Don't you think God knows her as well? And don't you think He is as forgiving?"

"Oh, *si, si!*" Theresa said. She crossed herself again. "*Si*, I think maybe you are right." She managed a smile through her tears then spoke to Munoz.

"Señor Munoz, creo que ahora la Señorita Locoste irá al cielo."

"Si, I think she will go to heaven," Munoz replied.

"I just cannot imagine who could do something like this," Polly said as she and Will returned to where Gid was standing.

Andrew Henson came into the parlor then. Polly knew that he was Marie's lawyer because, as Marie's accountant, she had discussed some business with him. Now he came over to see her.

"Mr. Henson, isn't it awful?" Polly asked.

"Yes, it is terrible," Henson agreed. He cleared his throat. "Miss Carpenter, I hate to bring up business at such a time, but I shall require your signature in at least half a dozen places. Perhaps we could go back into the dining room for a few moments? I'll lay all the papers out for you."

"My signature? What papers?"

"Oh, I'm sorry," Henson said. "You and Marie were so close, and of course you were handling most of her business. I just assumed you knew."

"Knew what, Mr. Henson?"

"About Marie's will, Miss Carpenter. Marie Lacoste named you as sole beneficiary to her entire estate. You have inherited all of her money, and the Carnation House."

Polly was so staggered by the news that her knees grew week and she had to grab hold of the table to keep from falling.

"Are you all right, Miss Carpenter?" Henson asked in concern, reaching out to hold her.

"Yes, I'm fine, I'm…I'm just stunned is all."

"There is a letter from Miss Lacoste," Henson said. "She asks that when you make the announcement to the others, that you read this letter to them."

Polly signed all the papers, but when she returned to the parlor, she didn't say anything to anyone about what had just happened.

It wasn't until after lunch when all the girls of Carnation House were sitting around in the parlor exchanging stories about Marie, most of them dealing with how they met her, when Polly asked if she could have their attention.

"I don't know how you are going to take what I have to say," she began hesitantly. "And I must confess that I haven't quite come to grips with it myself, as Mr. Henson just told me about it this morning."

"What is it, Polly?" Lucy asked.

Polly held up the letter. "This is a letter from Marie, to all of you."

"Read it to us," Lucy said.

Polly began to read.

To my dear daughters,

Yes, I know it is foolish of me to call you my daughters since I'm not old enough to have borne even the youngest of you; in mind, you truly are my daughters. I have left this letter to be read to you by Polly, in case anything happens to me, and no, I'm not expecting it, but this is just something I felt that I needed to do.

I have been asked from time to time, if I wouldn't have been happier in a profession that is more socially acceptable than that of the madam of a bordello. I always answer no, and those on the outside either don't believe me, or don't understand. My association with all of you has been a very happy one, and I wouldn't trade it for anything in the world.

And now for the business part of this letter. If something truly has happened to me, you may be worried as to your futures. Worry not. I have left Carnation House to Polly Carpenter and I know that she feels about you as I do, and I know that you all feel about her, as you do me.

I love each and every one of you, and I ask only that you keep me in your heart forever.

Marie

Polly folded the letter then looked into the face of each of the others.

"Oh, my God, how did she know something was going to happen to her?" Cathleen asked.

"She didn't know," Lucy said. "She was writin' the letter just in case."

"I have to ask you," Polly said. "I'm the newest one of you, so some of you may feel that it wasn't right for Marie to leave Carnation House to me."

"Polly, did you hear what you just said?" Lucy asked.

"Yes, I was asking how you feel about this."

Lucy smiled. "No, honey, you said you were the newest one of us. You don't consider yourself above or apart—you consider yourself one of us. And that is enough for me. I'm glad Marie left this place to you."

"You aren't going to sell it and leave us, are you?" Daisy asked.

Polly smiled. "I'm going to close it for business for the next three days out of respect for Marie. Then it will be business as usual."

"What about Lenny?" Lucy asked. "I know when he hears about this, he will want to come."

"Some of the others as well," Cathleen said.

"I said I would be closing it for business," Polly said. "It won't be closed to those who want to come and pay their respects."

Chapter Seventeen

Marie's funeral was conducted three days later. The procession to the cemetery was a stately affair that Polly felt certain would have pleased Marie. Marie's black and silver coffin rested behind the glass panels of the hearse, while two liveried coachmen drove a matching team of black horses to pull the funeral coach. People lined the streets on both sides, and they doffed their hats in respect as the procession passed them by.

Polly, Lucy, and the other girls from the Carnation House rode in two open carriages just behind the hearse. She and the others dabbed at their eyes openly and unashamedly as the solemn procession moved along the streets of the town.

The cemetery was a drab and dreary place. It was on a hill which overlooked the town of Shafter. It was completely barren, and grave sites were often marked by nothing more than a carpet of pebbles and rocks. Here and there were wooden head markers, but there were no granite monuments of the type which marked the graves of Marie's parents back in Memphis.

The grave had already been opened, the dirt alongside the hole white from the sun, though it had only been exposed for little more than an hour. The marker right next to the hole that was about to become Marie's grave, was that of Lucien Thompkins. It was not until Marie's will was read that the town found out a secret that Marie had kept all this time.

Marie Lacoste was actually Marie Thompkins, the widow of the man who had brought the theater group to Shafter, so long ago.

Those who had come to mourn at Marie's funeral now gathered around the grave as Father Tuttle, the Episcopal priest and the only clergyman in town who would agree to conduct the funeral of a harlot, began his graveside homily.

"It is," the Priest said, "perhaps fitting that this woman was known in life as Marie, for the name Marie, taken from Margaret, means 'woman of Magdala.' Once there was another woman of Magdala, a woman named Mary."

The Priest paused for a moment to allow his words to sink in. A hot breath of air moved through the cemetery, pushing before it a cloud of dust which stung the faces of the mourners.

"Like our Marie, Mary of Magdala was a locally notorious woman with a bad name in the town. But she came purposefully to make an act of penitence to Jesus, and she stood behind him at his feet, weeping so that she wet his feet with her tears. And she wiped his feet with the hair of her head, and she kissed his feet and then she anointed them with ointment.

"Now there was a Pharisee named Simon, in whose house this happened. Simon thought ill of the woman and he looked on in disapproval, but Jesus said to Simon, 'Do you see this woman? I entered your house, you gave me no water for my feet, but she has wet my feet with her tears, and wiped them with her hair. You gave me no kiss, but from the time I came in she has not ceased to kiss my feet. You did not anoint my head with oil, but she has anointed my feet with ointment. Therefore, I tell you, her sins, which are many, are forgiven, for she loved much, but he who loves little, is forgiven little.' And then Jesus said to Mary of Magdala, 'Your sins are forgiven. Your faith has saved you. Go in peace.'"

The priest looked at the coffin which contained Marie's body, and made the sign of the cross over it.

"Marie Lacoste, your sins are forgiven. The love you had for others has saved you. Go in peace."

Marie's coffin was lowered into the grave then, and the priest picked up a handful of dirt and dropped it into the grave. The dirt made a drumming sound as it hit on the lid of the casket.

"In sure and certain hope of the resurrection to eternal life through our Lord Jesus Christ, we commend to Almighty God our sister Marie Lacoste, and we commit her body to the ground; earth to earth, ashes to ashes, dust to dust.

The funeral ended shortly after that, and the mourners began returning to the horses, carriages, buggies and wagons that had brought them up here. Will and Gid had rented a buckboard and they invited Polly and Lucy to ride back with them. The remaining girls of Carnation House returned home in the same open carriage that had brought them. As they left, they could hear, behind them, the sound of the dirt leaving the spade as the hole was closed.

There was a brooding mood in Shafter. Will perceived it the moment they reached the edge of town. It was something he could sense in the air, like the heavy feel of the atmosphere just before a storm.

"Gid?" It was an unasked question, but Gid needed no more than the one word, for he understood.

"Yeah," Gid answered. "I know. Something is up."

"What is it?" Polly asked. "What are you two talking about?"

They saw two young boys running along the board sidewalk, jumping over the stoops and doorsills as they hurried toward the center of town."

"Hey, you boys! What's the hurry?" Will shouted.

"We're goin' to see the stretchin'!" one of the boys called back in excitement.

"Stretching?" Polly asked.

"Damn, there's a lynching goin' on!" Gid shouted. He was driving and he slapped the reins hard against the team to urge them into a gallop.

In no time the buckboard made it to the far end of the street, then, using his left foot, Gid pushed hard on the brake lever while he hauled back on the reins. The buckboard slid to a stop.

"Ole' Munoz never looked so good," someone on the edge of the crowd said in a high, nervous voice. Someone else giggled.

"What is it?" Will asked. "What's going on here?"

The crowd began parting to allow Will and the others to pass through. When he got to the front of the crowd, he saw what had drawn them here. Señor Munoz was hanging from a crosspiece that had been nailed between two telegraph poles. The old cook's hands were tied behind his back and his neck was grotesquely stretched out of shape. He had not been blindfolded and his eyes were open, as if staring accusingly at his lynchers. The rope creaked as Munoz swung slowly back and forth on the makeshift gallows.

"My God!" Polly said, putting her hand over her mouth. "Who did this?"

"A group of Marie's friends," someone in the crowd answered. "Munoz killed Marie so they hung him up for it."

"You are mad, all of you," Lucy said. "Señor Munoz would never do such a thing! He loved Marie!"

Will and Gid said nothing more as they drove Polly and Lucy back to the Carnation House. Letting them out there, they then drove down to the Jingle Bob Corral, where they turned in the buckboard and the team. From there, they walked across the street to the Dust Cutter Saloon.

"Yes, sir," Townsend was saying. He put his finger to the side of his head. "I started thinkin' on it, and I got it all figured out."

"So, you decided to kill Munoz yourself, is that it?" Will asked.

"You damn right I ..." Townsend started to answer, but when he saw that Will was the one who asked the question, he clammed up. "Crockett," he said, "what are you doing here?"

"I'm going to throw your ass in jail," Will said. "And you're going to stay there for about three days."

"Three days," Townsend snorted. "And what's going to happen in three days?"

"We're going to see another hanging," Will replied. "Only this time it's going to be legal."

"Who do you think you're kidding?" Townsend asked. "You ain't goin' to be able to put together a jury in this town that will hang me for what I done. Hell, half of 'em was out there, eggin' me on!"

"Then I'll hang you myself," Will said, flatly. "Either way, you're going to hang."

"The hell I am!" Townsend shouted. He pulled his gun, even as he was shouting his defiance. Will had not yet pulled his gun, but Townsend had his out and was coming back on the hammer even as Will started for his pistol. Will turned as he drew, presenting a sideways profile, rather than the broader, front profile. That action saved his life, for Townsend pulled the trigger at about the same time Will was bringing his own gun up, and the bullet missed Will by less than an inch. Had Will been in a full-frontal presentation, the bullet would have hit him in the heart.

Townsend thumbed the hammer back for a second shot, already correcting for his error, when Will fired.

Will's bullet crashed into Townsend's heart, killing him so quickly that he was dead before he hit the floor.

"Drop your gun, Crockett!" a loud voice called.

Looking into the recently replaced mirror behind the bar, Will saw Sheriff Jones and Deputy Sheriff Gentry. Both men were holding shotguns, and the guns were pointed at Will and Gid.

"What's this about?" Will asked.

"I said, *drop the gun*!" Jones repeated. "You too" he added, talking to Gid. "Unbuckle your gunbelt. There will be no more taking the law into your own hands."

"Where were you this afternoon when this son of a bitch lynched Munoz?" Will asked.

"Lynched Munoz? Far as I'm concerned, he just saved the county the cost of a legal hanging'," Jones said. "He was right. Munoz was the killer."

"How do you know that?"

"Because I seen him comin' out of the whorehouse around two o'clock in the mornin' on the night Marie Lacoste was killed," Gentry said.

"That proves nothing. He worked there."

"He was a cook. He had no business bein' there at that time of night," Jones said.

"He also lived there," Will said. "Anyway, even if he did do it, and I know damn well he didn't, Townsend had no right to hang him."

"I know that," Jones said. "That's why we came over here. We was goin' to arrest him and put him on trial. But we got here too late. You'd already killed him. So now we'll just put you on trial."

"Don't worry, Will," Henry Deer said. "They's enough of us in here seen what really happened, when Judge Newcomb hears our side of it, he'll let you go in minute."

"Let's go," Jones said, making a motion with his shotgun. "You know what I think I'm goin' to do? I'm goin' to lock you up in the county jail." He laughed. "Yeah, I like that. Town Marshals Will and Gid Crockett, locked up in the county jail."

"What about the others?" Will asked.

"What others?"

"The others who helped Townsend kill Munoz. You don't think he did it by himself, do you?"

"Yeah, well, we'll look into it," Sheriff Jones said.

Townsend was buried the next afternoon. Will stood at the side window of the cell, the only window that afforded a view of the street and watched as the hearse rolled slowly toward the cemetery.

Moe Tucker, Isaac and Amos McAfee, and two dozen or more cowboys walked along behind the hearse, all of them wearing a black mourning band around their arms.

"I'll be damned," Gid said. "Look at that." He pointed to a sign on the hearse.

Asa P. Townsend,

A Cowboy foully murdered

by

Will Crockett.

Chapter Eighteen

"Townsend was one of our cowboys, and you didn't even bother to come to his funeral," Moe said, chastising his brother.

"Yes, well as far as I'm concerned Townsend and the others who helped him lynch poor old Munoz were nothing but murderers," Lenny said.

"They were just saving the county the bother of a trial and the cost of a hangin'," Moe said.

"Munoz didn't murder Miss Lacoste."

"How do you know?"

"Because I knew Munoz, and I know that he would never have done that. He loved Miss Lacoste."

"Oh, yeah, I'd almost forgotten. My brother has always been welcomed at the whorehouse, while the bitch that ran it didn't want anything to do with me."

"Maybe if you showed a little more consideration for

people you would be welcome."

"I see no need to show any consideration for Marie Lacoste or any other whore who spreads her legs there," Moe said. "And that includes the whore you're so thick with."

"Careful what you say about Lucy," Lenny said.

"Why? She's no different from any of the other whores except maybe she's a little better lookin'."

"I'll tell you something different about her," Lenny said. "If she'll have me, I'm going to marry her."

Judge Newcomb set Will and Gid's trial for one week later, and on the day of the trial, two men who were to have a role to play arrived on the morning train. One of the two men was J. Warren Beck, a prosecuting attorney known throughout the West as the man who prosecuted cases in Judge Isaac Charles Parker's Federal Court at Fort Smith, Arkansas. Judge Parker's swift justice had resulted in so many hangings that he became known far and wide as "the hanging judge." That reputation rested somewhat on the successful prosecution of the cases that came before him, and that prosecution had been carried out by J. Warren Beck.

Warren Beck dressed in a three-piece suit and carried a silver-headed cane. He wore a diamond stickpin in his tie, solid gold cufflinks, and a gold watch chain stretching across the silk vest that did little to conceal his substantial girth. Like his mentor, Judge Parker, he had affected a Van Dyke beard. He kept his hair cut short, and neatly combed.

The other person to arrive was George Maledon, and whenever he entered a town, mothers shuddered and pulled their children close to them.

Maledon was a very small, full-bearded man who always carried a brace of hand-woven, well-oiled, expensive Kentucky hemp ropes with him. He was a professional hangman who had carried out more than fifty death sentences and had been dubbed "the prince of hangmen."

Though Sheriff Jones had arrested Will and Gid, Doc had persuaded Judge Newcomb to move them from the county jail, which was under Jones's administration, to the town jail. And, because Will and Gid were the town marshals, Newcomb managed to get U.S. Marshal Ephraim Weaver brought in to take charge of the prisoners until the trial.

When Andrew Henson walked into the jail shortly after the prosecutor and the hangman arrived, he saw Will, Doc, Gid, and Marshal Weaver sitting around a card table, playing poker.

"Mr. Henson," Weaver said. "Have you ever played poker with this man?" He nodded toward Will.

"I can't say that I have," Henson replied.

"I think he cheats," Weaver said. "I think we ought to put him in jail."

"I *am* in jail," Will said, laughing.

"Oh, yes, so you are." Weaver said. "Well, good enough for you. I fold."

Will took the hand and raked in the pot, which consisted of a dozen or more matches. He looked over at Henson and smiled. "How goes the fight for justice?" he asked.

"It may be more difficult than we thought," Henson answered.

"How can it be? Self-defense is self-defense."

"Beck has witnesses who will testify that you once shot Townsend in the foot without provocation. Did you?"

"Hell no, I was plenty provoked," Will replied, and he, Gid, and Doc laughed.

Henson cleared his throat. "Yes, well, according to Beck, that created such an atmosphere of fear and distrust that Townsend could never be sure, any time he saw you, but what you might shoot him again. Thus, as he believed his life was in danger, he was fully justified in drawing against you."

"Well, all right, justified or not, he drew against me first."

Henson shook his head. "No," he said. "If Beck proves his case, your very presence was enough of a threat to make Townsend fear for his life. Thus, you are the aggressor. And as the aggressor, you are guilty of murder."

"What about Gid? He didn't do anything."

"They will get him for aiding and abetting," Henson said.

Will drummed his fingers on the table. "Well," he said. "Thanks for coming to cheer me up."

"There's uh, more," Henson said.

"Bye all means, let's have all of it."

"You'll have to leave the jail to see it."

"Hell, that's no problem for me," Will said, smiling broadly. "I'd be glad to leave the jail."

With U.S. Marshal Ephraim Weaver acting as the guard, and with their word of honor as their only restraint, Will and Gid left the jail and walked with Doc, Henson, and the U.S. marshal to see what Henson had to show them.

It was a hangman's gallows.

There were a couple dozen people were standing around watching the construction. A large, hand-lettered sign stood in front of the gallows:

On this Gallows, The Master Executioner,

George Maledon,

"The Prince Of Hangmen"

Will Hang

Will Crockett

and

Gid Crockett.

These Two Murderers Will Be

Prosecuted by J. Warren Beck

And Legally Sent To Meet Their Maker

Admission is Free.

Moe Tucker was supervising the construction of the gallows. A ladder of thirteen steps led up to the gallows floor which was made of freshly cut one-by-eight-inch planks. The tree of the gallows was constructed of four-by-four timbers—three uprights and one crosspiece at the top. Two ropes hung from the crosstree, one on either side of the center brace. The ropes were made of twenty strands of the finest hemp, one-and-a-half inches in circumference. Sandbags were tied to the ropes and two chairs had been placed invitingly on the twenty-foot square with a placard on each chair, one for Will Crockett and the other for Gid Crockett.

The platform looked solid, but Will could see that it had two ominous divisions which were supported by upright timbers. When those timbers were knocked out of place, the front part of the platform would swing down on hinges and feet of anyone who had been standing there would be left dangling in midair, the falls broken only by a rope around the neck.

At this moment there were two one-hundred-pound weights on the platform. Moe stepped back from the edge.

"Okay, try it!" Moe shouted.

The two muscular men beneath the platform swung heavy hammers at the supporting posts. The posts were knocked away and the long, narrow trap fell open. The two weights dropped for a short distance, then were jerked up short by the rope.

Seeing Will and Gid, Moe bounded down the steps. He called out to them. "Hey, Crocketts! Come to see your gallows, did you? How do you like it?"

"What are you doing here, Tucker?" Marshal Weaver asked.

"Why, I'm doing my civic duty," Moe said. He took in the gallows with a wave of his hand. "I have volunteered to foot all the expenses of the hangin'. I'm the one brought Maledon in here. I'm payin' him two hundred and fifty dollars per neck, plus all his expenses."

"You have no right to build this damn thing, or to bring in a hangman," Weaver said.

"I'm rentin' this empty lot," Moe said. "That makes me the proprietor, and I can build any kind of construction here that I want. I choose to build a gallows."

"You are inflaming the passions of the people," Henson said.

"You're damn right I'm inflaming' the passions of the

people," Tucker replied. "That's what I was a' plannin' on doin'. I aim to see these two men pay for killin' one o' my cowboys. Why, what kind of rancher would I be, if I didn't look out for my own men?"

"If you'd really been looking out for Townsend, you wouldn't have let him murder Señor Munoz."

"That Mex got what he deserved for murderin' an innocent woman," one of the bystanders said.

Will recognized him as Allen Jensen, owner of Jensen's Mercantile.

"Jensen, you hypocritical bastard, two weeks ago you wouldn't even let that innocent woman come to a square dance the town held," Gid said.

"Yeah, well, uh, that doesn't mean I don't think who-ever killed her shouldn't have been hanged."

At that moment Deputy Gentry came toward them and he pointed to Will and Gid.

"Marshal, what do you mean letting those two mur-derers out of jail? They got no right to be walkin' around free like this. That's puttin' all the good people in a lot of danger."

"They aren't free, they're under my supervision," Marshal Weaver replied. "And speaking of doing your duty how is it that you let this man build a gallows even before the trial has been held?"

Gentry smiled. "It's just like Moe said. He's rented

this land so he can build anything on it he wants. Besides, he's payin' for it all his ownself, 'n that's savin' the county some money."

"I'll get a court order to have it taken down," Henson said.

"Hell, that don't make any difference to me," Moe said. "Ever' one's seen it by now. And if I have to take it down, I'll just leave it in pieces so it can be put back together again, real easy. Besides, you can't get no court order to have Maledon run out of town, and ever' where he goes people will see him 'n they'll know why he's here."

"Let him leave it up," Will said. "When this is all over, I might use it to hang *him*."

When he heard Will's calm words, the smile left Moe's face.

Chapter Nineteen

"*Oyez, oyez, oyez*, the Circuit Court of Persidio County in the State of Texas is now in session, the Honorable Judge Wells Newcomb presiding. All rise!"

Everyone in the courtroom rose as the judge emerged from his chambers and walked over to the bench. When he was seated, the gallery was invited to sit as well and there was a rustle of clothes and a squeak of boots and shoes as the spectators got themselves settled. The courtroom was packed. Admission had been granted on a first-come, first-seated basis, and some people had been outside the courtroom since before dawn.

Polly was in the first row of the gallery, and Lucy and Doc were sitting with her. Also sitting in the same row, but on the other side of the center aisle, were Moe and Lenny Tucker, Isaac and Amos McAfee, and a handful of witnesses who were going to testify for the prosecution.

Will and Gid were seated at the defendants' table with their lawyer, Andrew Henson.

Judge Newcomb removed his wire-rimmed glasses and polished them industriously for a moment, holding them up to the light of the window and staring through the lenses, then polishing them even more vigorously. During this ritual of cleaning and polishing there was total silence in the court. Finally, Judge Newcomb deemed his glasses clean enough, or perhaps he just considered the mood in the court somber enough, because he put his glasses back on, hooking them very carefully over one ear at a time. Then he fixed a long, studied stare upon the courtroom and cleared his throat.

"The State of Texas versus Will Crockett and Gideon Crockett," he said. "Is the prosecution ready?"

J. Warren Beck stood, put one hand inside his silk vest, then looked over toward the jury.

"Ready, Your Honor," he said in a deep, resonant voice.

"Is the defense ready?'

"Yes, Your Honor," Henson replied, half rising from his chair.

Beck began to make his case then, using a parade of witnesses who testified as to the demeanor of the town marshals. Witnesses testified that Will had killed Ernest Fowler and Leo Bell on the very first day they had arrived in town, and though they conceded that it was a fair fight, they said it was a demonstration not only of the marshal's skill with a gun, but of his willingness to kill.

They testified that the Crocketts had immediately become friendly with Doc Hawkins, the only other person in town with sufficient skill with a gun to act as a balance to the reign of terror the Crocketts had brought upon the town.

Witnesses also testified that Will and Gid Crockett, as well as Doc Hawkins, had harassed, threatened, and beaten Moe Tucker and Isaac and Amos McAfee.

"I object, Your Honor. This testimony is irrelevant," Henson said.

"On the contrary, Your Honor," Beck defended. "It is all part and parcel of the picture I am painting of the marshals, Will and Gid Crockett. It is validation of the fact that the behavior of these two men was brutal and profane, even with men of position and wealth. And if that is so, then how much more ruthless and debasing could it be to a poor cowboy of no consequence, such as Asa Townsend?"

"Objection overruled," Judge Newcomb said. "You may continue."

Beck's next witness was Sheriff Jones, who testified not about the shooting, but about the night Asa Townsend, Moe Tucker and Isaac and Amos McAfee tried to enter the Carnation House, only to be stopped by Will, Gid, and Doc.

"And when you arrived on the scene to bring order to what was obviously a volatile situation, there was an exchange between you and the defendant, Will Crockett. Would you share that conversation with the court?"

"'Be glad to," Jones replied. "Crockett asked me why did I butt in? I told him, 'Hell, somebody had to take a hand. Things was startin' to get out of control.' He said. 'Yeah, well, I was about to put things back into control.' I asked him how did he plan to do that?"

"And what was his answer?" Beck asked.

Sheriff Jones looked over at the defendants' table.

"He said, just as calm and cold as if it was nothin', 'I was goin' to kill them'," Jones answered.

There was a collective gasp of surprise from the court as Beck walked back over to his own table and shuffled through a few papers before calling his last witness.

The last witness for the prosecution testified about the night that Will had shot Townsend in the foot. Nothing was mentioned about Townsend's previously threatening to kill Señor Munoz.

"I have no further witnesses, Your Honor," Beck said, sitting down after he excused the final witness.

There was another collective gasp of surprise from those in the court. Beck had called witnesses who testified about three months of events and behavior, but he did not call one person to give testimony about the actual shooting in which Townsend was killed.

Now it was time for the defense attorney to make his case. Henson called his own parade of witnesses to the stand, matching the prosecution's witness, man for man. Whereas all of Beck's witnesses had been cowboys, Henson called only those men who lived and worked in the town. Among Henson's witnesses were the mayor and two members of the town council, all of whom told the court that they had gone to ask Will and Gid Crockett to take the job of town marshal.

"And are you sorry you asked them, now?" Henson asked. He asked the same question of all three, and all three answered the same way.

"I am not in the least sorry. They have been fine marshals and I believe their presence has prevented more than one drunken cowboy from trying to settle his argument with guns or knives."

"You have heard testimony that there has been a systematic pattern of mistreatment against the ranchers and their riders," Henson asked. "It is true, is it not, that Moe Tucker has spent at least six nights in jail since the Crocketts pinned on their badges?"

"Yes. At least six nights."

"And the McAfees at least five?"

"Yes."

"In your opinion, Mr. Mayor, does that validate Mr. Beck's contention that he was picking on them?"

"No, sir, it does not," Malone answered. "In every case, the Crocketts showed amazing forbearance. On more than one of those occasions, a less confident law enforcement officer might have felt a need to resort to guns. The Crocketts did not."

Henry Deer, the bartender of the Dust Cutter, testified that on the night Will shot Townsend in the foot, Townsend had been menacing the entire saloon with a loaded weapon, all the more frightening because he was the only one armed that night, due to a one-night-only ordinance prohibiting the carrying of guns. He had also threatened to kill Munoz on that night.

Finally, Henson had six witnesses from the saloon who testified that Will had no choice but to shoot Townsend on the night he was killed. All six swore that Will had given Townsend an opportunity to surrender but that Townsend had pulled his gun and shot, even managing to get off the first shot before Will killed him.

"If Marshal Crockett had not turned sideways like he done, that bullet would'a kilt him sure," one of the witnesses said.

When the final witness's testimony was heard, Henson walked over to face the jurors. The lawyer turned and pointed to Will and Gid.

"We have asked these men to stand between us and those who would rob us, beat us, and kill us," he said. "The prosecutor has painted a picture that is totally false. He claims that Will and Gid Crockett harassed, abused, and mistreated Moe Tucker and Isaac and Amos McAfee, who were nothing more than defenseless cattlemen.

"But I would point out to you that these same 'defenseless' cattlemen killed Dan Rankin and five of his riders in a deadly, night gun battle. And I would also point out to you that Lenny Tucker, Moe's own brother and one of the cattlemen with whom Beck claims the Crocketts have an ongoing feud, has never been arrested, or harassed in any way. Why is this? Because Lenny Tucker has not violated any laws or ordinances.

"Moe Tucker, Isaac and Amos McAfee, and yes, Asa Townsend were frequent violators of laws, ordinances, and just plain common decency. It is no secret that these men were not, and that they are not welcome in the Carnation House."

"Well, I never ..." one woman in the gallery said, self-righteously.

"And if Carnation House is a place of questionable repute that is all the more reason to hold these men in contempt for their boorish behavior. It is just such behavior that put them at odds with marshals Will and Gid Crockett and that is as it should be, for such was the task we, as citizens, laid out for the Crocketts to perform.

"It was not some blood lust, then, that brought about the fatal confrontation in the Dust Cutter Saloon that night. It was, quite simply, a brave man's performance of duty."

Will and Gid both nodded at Henson when he sat down, indicating that they appreciated what he had said and done for them.

Now Beck rose from his seat. He opened his watch, looked at it, then snapped it shut and put it back into his vest pocket.

"I submit to you, gentlemen of the jury, that every man has his breaking point. The weakest and the most cowardly among us can be pushed to a point at which we will turn and fight. Asa Townsend was not weak or cowardly, but he was foolish. He was foolish to let a professional gunman goad him into drawing against him.

"I have done some research on these men whom you have hired as your town marshals. During the war they rode not under the Stars and Stripes of the United States, nor even under the Stars and Bars of the Confederacy. Instead, they chose to give their allegiance to the black flag of Quantrill. It is not known how many men they killed during that war, though an estimate of twenty apiece would not be out of hand. Since then they have cut a swath of death and destruction across the Southwest, killing, robbing, and staying just ahead of the wanted posters until they arrived here, where their crimes had not yet caught up with them.

"How many men had Asa Townsend killed? The answer, my friends is one, and one only. He killed, in an act of understandable rage, the monster who killed Miss Marie Lacoste. Had Townsend not killed Munoz, it is for sure and certain that a legally constituted court would have sentenced Munoz to death. Townsend's killing of Munoz was wrong then, not because of the act, but because of the timing.

"And finally, I ask you to consider the testimony of defense's own witnesses. They testified that Townsend fired first, and we will concede that. He fired first in reaction to the sure and certain knowledge that Will Crockett was going to kill him. Consider the picture their witnesses painted for you. Townsend, terrified, fired first, his bullet going wide of the mark. Will Crockett, calm, collected, and cold-blooded, stands unflinching in the face of Asa Townsend's blazing pistol and returns fire. It takes but one shot and Townsend is dead.

"One shot and Ernest Fowler is dead.

"One shot and Leo Bell is dead.

"Was it really self-defense as the defendant claims? Or was it a cold, calculated murder, the result of intentionally goading the victim into his irrational reaction?"

"He's good," Doc said in unabashed admiration for the prosecutor. "I've never in my life heard anyone who could do such a good job of turning a heroic action into cold-blooded murder."

"Oh, Doc!" Polly said. "You don't think they will find Will and Gid guilty, do you?"

Doc chuckled. "No. There is an old adage among lawyers: 'When you have evidence, use evidence. When you don't have evidence, use fancy words.' Fancy words are all he had."

"I hope and pray that you are right," Polly said.

The jury deliberated for twenty minutes, then someone saw them leave the deliberation room and shouted to the others. "The jury is comin' back!"

The jury filed in and sat down, trying not to give away the decision by the expressions on their faces. Judge Newcomb returned to the court and called it to order.

"Mr. Foreman, have you reached a verdict?"

"We have, Your Honor."

"Would the defendants and their counsel please stand?"

Will, Gid, and Henson stood. Behind them, Will could hear the collective pause of breath while the gallery waited.

"What is your verdict?" Judge Newcomb asked.

The foreman looked directly at Will and Gid.

"We find the defendants Will Crockett and Gideon

Crockett ... not guilty," the foreman said.

"Good job, Henson!" Doc shouted from the gallery. The court exploded into shouts, some of joy, some of anger. Polly, Lucy, and Doc pushed through the rail to reach them and Doc shook their hands, then stepped back, smiling, as Polly and Lucy gave them a much more personal congratulations.

"Crockett!" Moe shouted from the other side of the courtroom.

Will and Gid both looked toward Moe.

"It ain't over, Crockett!" Moe said, pointing menacingly toward them. "It ain't over!"

Chapter Twenty

Moe Tucker took a room at the Del Rey Hotel but he needn't have bothered. The only bed he saw that night was one of the crib whores, and that bed wasn't for sleeping.

After Moe left the whore's bed, he decided to make a long, sodden night of it; he sat at a table in the back of the Dust Cutter sullenly downing shot after shot of whiskey until well past midnight.

At around one o'clock in the morning he decided to get something to eat. The café he chose happened to be occupied by Will and Gid Crockett, but they didn't seem to notice him. He chose a table in the back and ordered a fried ham sandwich.

About halfway through his sandwich, Doc Hawkins came in, saw Moe, and went over to his table. "You son of a bitch, you tried to railroad two good men," Doc said angrily. "Pull your gun."

"I've got no quarrel with you."

"Well I've got one with you, you back-shooting bastard!" Doc said. "The Crocketts are my friends and you tried to do them in."

Will heard the commotion and he looked over toward him.

"Doc," he called easily. "Let him be."

"I'll let him be," Doc said. "When he's six feet under, I'll let him be."

"I said let him be," Will said again, and Doc, still muttering, left the café.

"That man's crazy," Moe said. "Someone ought to lock him up."

"Moe, why don't you finish your sandwich and go on to bed before there's trouble?" Will suggested.

"I'll go where I damn well please," Moe replied.

After the meal Moe left the café, not to go to bed, but to return to the Dust Cutter Saloon. He drank right through until sunrise the next day.

The next morning, out at the Tucker Ranch, Lenny went into the dining room for breakfast. The cook had already started the coffee, and its rich aroma filled the kitchen. Lenny wandered into the kitchen and poured himself a cup, then leaned against the sideboard, drinking the coffee and watching the cook prepare breakfast.

"Moe up yet?" Lenny asked.

"Your brother no' come home last night," the cook said.

"He didn't come home? Are you sure?"

"*Si*, I am sure. I go into his room to tell him that soon, breakfast will be ready, but he is not in his room and his bed is not ..." She made a rotary motion with her hand to indicate that the bed had not been mussed.

Lenny picked up a golden-brown biscuit from a pan and took a bite from it.

"Then I guess I'd better go into town and see if I can find him, before he gets into trouble," he said. "If it's not already too late."

"I know you are always the one who wants to move on and I'm the one who gets a hankering to stay," Gid said to Will. "But I tell you true, Big Brother, I've about had it with this place."

The two brothers had just finished breakfast and were walking back to the marshal's office.

"I know you're feeling bad about Marie—I do too," Will said. "And ordinarily, I'd be agreeing with you. But I'd sort of hate to leave the town in the lurch right now, especially after the way they all stood up for us at that trial."

"Well, I can see that. The thing I'm wonderin' is, just how long are you planning' on stayin' around?"

"I don't know," Will answered, "but I don't think it

will be much longer. I've got a feeling that things will be coming to a head around here soon."

"You're talking about Tucker and the McAfees, aren't you?"

"Yes," Will answered. "We can't leave now, Gid. Not with this situation unsettled. It would be like running away and it would haunt us both, for the rest of our lives."

"Yeah," Gid said. "I reckon there's some truth to that."

As Will and Gid were on their way to the marshal's office, Lenny Tucker was just arriving in Shafter, and he stopped in front of the general store, where he saw the proprietor sweeping off the store's front porch.

"Have you seen my brother, Mr. Moore?" he asked.

"Not since yesterday, Lenny," Moore answered. "I'm sorry."

"Thanks anyway. I'll find him."

Lenny tied off his horse and started walking toward the Del Rey Hotel.

"Mornin', Lenny," someone said as he passed Lenny on the board sidewalk.

"Good mornin' to you," Lenny said. "Say, have you seen Moe this morning?"

"Matter of fact, I have," the passerby said. "He's over at the Hermitage having his breakfast."

"Thanks," Lenny said.

Lenny left the sidewalk and crossed the dirt street,

picking his way gingerly through the horse droppings. He pushed the door open at the Hermitage Café and saw Moe sitting at a table in the back. It was all Moe could do to hold his head up. Lenny walked back to the table and sat down.

"Lenny, boy," Moe said, grinning broadly. "I knew you'd come. I knew you wouldn't let your old brother down."

"Look at you," Lenny said. "Did you even go to bed last night?"

"Last night?" Moe said. He hiccupped, then smiled. "Last night ain't over yet." He pointed toward the front window. "Oh, it might be light out but the night ain't over 'till it's over, if you know what I mean."

"You're so damn drunk I don't think *you* even know what you mean," Lenny said.

The waitress brought a plate of eggs, potatoes and fried ham to set before Moe. Moe looked at it stupidly for a moment, as if having difficulty making his eyes focus. Then he smiled.

"Oh, yeah," he said, grinning. "I was sittin' here waitin' on another drink, but I must've ordered breakfast by mistake." He looked at Lenny. "Want some?"

"I ate at home."

"Oh, yeah, I forgot," Moe said. "You're the good boy." Moe put a forkful of eggs into his mouth, and the yellow dribbled down his chin and dripped onto his shirt. His shirt was already stained with whiskey, perfume, powder, and rouge from his night of carousing. "I remember before Pa and Hilda died. They both thought I should be more like you. Tell me, Lenny, do you think I should be more like you?"

"Would it do any good if I said I thought you should?"

"It might," Moe said. "Course, first I got me this little score to settle with the Crocketts. But you know that, 'cause you come to town to help me out."

"Moe, come on," Lenny said. "Let's go back home."

"I'll go back after I've settled accounts with the Crocketts," Moe said.

"Let it be, Moe. They had their day in court and it's all over now. We've got more important things to worry about than the Crocketts."

"No!" Moe shouted. He stood up and leaned over the table, using his fork to point at Lenny. The others in the restaurant looked over nervously.

"Moe, sit down," Lenny said quietly.

To Lenny's surprise, Moe did sit down. But he didn't quit talking. "There ain't nothin' more important than standin' up like a man," he said. "You hear me, Lenny? Now, what's it goin' to be? Are you goin' to stand up like a man? Or are you goin' to turn coward and run?"

"Moe, I don't have a quarrel with the Crocketts."

"Well, by God I do!" Moe said. "And if you're really my brother ... my fight is your fight."

"Let it go, Moe."

"No!" Moe shouted, slamming his fist onto the table with such force that his knife and fork bounced onto the floor.

"You're making a scene," Lenny cautioned.

"I don't care. This here thing with the Crocketts has gone far enough. We're goin' to settle it today, once and for all."

"You aren't in any condition to settle anything," Lenny said. "Look at you. Hell, you can't even stand up."

"If the Crocketts call me out today, are you goin' to back me up? Or, are you goin' to turn tail and run?"

"It won't come to that."

Moe pulled himself together and stared intently into Lenny's face. "It might. They're killers, Lenny, both of them. You heard what they said about them in court. They rode with Quantrill. No tellin' how many men they kilt when they was with Quantrill. Hell, there's no tellin' how many men they've kilt since then. They might call me out. And if they do, Lenny, what I want to know is, will you back me up?"

Lenny sighed. "You're my brother, Moe. Of course if it comes to that I will back you up."

Moe grinned broadly. "I was hopin' you'd say that,"

he said. "Just knowin' I can count on you makes me happy. He put his arm around Lenny's shoulder and started for the door. "Come on."

"Where are we going?"

"We're goin' home," Moe said. He laughed. "If the Crocketts want to have a shootout, why, they can just have it amongst themselves."

Lenny laughed happily. "Now you're making sense."

Chapter Twenty-One

Deputy Gentry was at the boot repair shop to get a new heel put on his spare pair of boots when he saw Lenny and Moe. Earlier he had seen the McAfees down at the Jingle Bob Corral. Everyone knew that a showdown was coming between the Crocketts and the cowboys anyway, so why not now?

If he could get rid of the Crockett brothers, he was sure that he would be able to use his position as deputy sheriff to act as the town marshal. And as town marshal, he would be able to find opportunities to make money. Maybe there was some way he could move the showdown up.

Lenny was leading his horse and Moe was walking alongside, heading for the Jingle Bob Corral where he had put up his horse for the night.

Gentry watched for just a minute, then putting his boots down, he ran to catch up with Moe and Lenny.

"Wait!" Gentry shouted, holding out his hand to stop them. He was badly out of breath from the run and leaned against the wall, his chest heaving, as he breathed in ragged gasps.

"Well, if it isn't my friend Roscoe Gentry," Moe said. When he saw how out of breath Gentry was, he walked back toward him. "What the hell is wrong with you?" he asked. "Why are you so out of breath?"

"I had to run to catch you in time to warn you," Gentry said.

"Warn me about what?"

"The Crocketts. They're going to be waiting for you boys when you leave town today," Gentry said as he expanded on his lie to make certain that the fight would happen. "They're telling it all over that they intend to end this feud between you, once and for all. They're going to bushwhack you."

"By God, I can believe that," Moe said. "Bushwhackers they were, and bushwhacker they are." He turned to look toward his brother. "Did you hear that, Lenny? Now, what do you think?"

"Come on, Moe, let's get out of here before something happens," Lenny said.

"No! Hell no! You said if the time ever came, you'd be standin' beside me," Moe said. He walked back over to Lenny and held his finger in Lenny's face. "Well, brother, it's down to the nut-cutting," he said. "The time is here, now."

"Moe, do you know what you're talking about here? You're talking about going up against men who can kill as easily as they sneeze. We aren't like them."

"You, maybe. You ain't never killed anyone," Moe said. "But I have. And believe me, Little Brother, there's nothing to it. It ain't the big thing it's made out to be."

"Gentry, are you sure about that? Have you actually heard them say that they plan to ambush us on our way home?"

"I heard it more 'n once," Gentry said. "Even though they wasn't found guilty, they still got a mad on ag'in Moe here, on account of he built that gallows 'n all."

"How come they aren't mad at you and Sheriff Jones? You're the ones who arrested them?" Lenny asked.

"They ain't all that mad at us, 'cause they know we was just doin' our duty. It's Moe they're wantin' to kill."

"Then why don't you arrest them?"

"I can't arrest 'em now, on account of they ain't done nothin'. I can arrest 'em after they've kilt you 'n Moe, only thing is, then it would be too late for you two. I'm just doin' my duty now to warn you so you can defend yourselves."

"What do you say now, Lenny?" Moe asked.

Lenny swallowed. "All right," he said. "I told you I'd

be there for you and I will be."

"It's not going to be as hard as you think," Moe said. "Isaac and Amos have been waitin' for this opportunity. They're in town. We'll get them first, then we'll get this thing settled. There will be four of us and two of them. I think we'll be all right."

"There will be five of us," Gentry said.

Moe and Lenny looked at Gentry in surprise. "Five of us?" Moe asked. "But you're the deputy sheriff."

Gentry nodded. "I am, but I consider you boys my friends," he said. "When the shootin' starts, I plan to be there."

Moe smiled broadly and reached out to take Gentry's hand. "You are a good man, Roscoe," he said. "I always knew that."

"If you want my opinion, I think we should just go home," Amos McAfee said when Moe, Lenny, and Gentry found them and told them that they planned to settle this today, once and for all. They were holding the conversation around the watering trough out front of the barn at the Jingle Bob Corral. Both the front and back doors of the barn were open to allow air in to cool the horses. A light breeze was blowing through from the opposite side of the barn carrying on its breath the sweetly pungent smell of horses and manure.

To the right of the door were parked the half-dozen buckboards and wagons the stable had for rent. The stable owner, a man everyone called Muley, was working on the wheel of one of the wagons, though he was far enough away from the five men that he couldn't hear what they were discussing.

"We can't go home, Amos," Isaac said. "Moe is right. We've got to have this thing out now. If we don't, we ain't ever goin' to have any peace around here."

"Yeah, well, if we go up against the Crocketts we'll have peace all right. But the only peace some of us are going to have is eternal peace," Amos said. He looked at Lenny. "Lenny, you're generally the sanest one of us all. I can't believe you're ready for this."

"I don't want it," Lenny said. He sighed. "But I'm afraid it's gone too far now. Gentry overheard them planning to ambush us when we leave town. The day I've been dreading is here, and there's nothing we can do about it but play it out."

"Damn," Amos said. Suddenly, and incongruously, he laughed.

"What is it?" Isaac asked. "What are you laughin' at?"

"Peaches."

"Peaches?"

"That can of peaches I near about bought while ago? I wish now I had bought it."

"Why?"

"'Cause I really love canned peaches, and it might'a been my last chance to ever have any," Amos said. "I don't figure the devil will be servin' 'em in hell."

They were quiet for a moment, then Moe growled. "We goin' to stand around and talk all day? Or are we goin' to get this thing done?"

"Let's get it done," Isaac said.

"Wait," Lenny called. The others turned to look at him.

"If we're goin' to do this, let's make them come to us," he suggested. "That way, we'll have the advantage. And when it's over, there won't be no question about it bein' murder or anything."

"Yeah, good idea," Moe said. He smiled. "I always knowed that Lenny was the smartest one of us all. Muley," he called.

Responding to the call, Muley got up from the wagon wheel and walked over toward them, wiping his hands with a rag he carried in his back pocket.

"Yes, Mr. Tucker?"

"Muley, we want you to do something for us," Moe said. As he was talking, he took out his pistol and began checking the loads in the cylinder. That reminded the others of the necessity of being prepared, so they did the same thing.

"What?" Muley asked, his eyes growing wide at the

sight of five men checking their pistols. "What's going on, here?"

"We're about to settle accounts," Moe said. "We want you to go down to the marshal's office and tell them we're waitin' for 'em down here."

"You're going to shoot it out with the Crocketts?"

"That's right," Moe said.

Muley shook his head. "You boys don't really want to do that," he said, his voice high-pitched and nervous.

"Yeah," Moe said, looking pointedly at him. "We do. Now, you go down there and get them like we said. Then you stay the hell out of the way."

"And tell the others to stay away too," Lenny said. "No need in getting any innocent people killed."

Isaac laughed. "Your brother's just real thoughtful, ain't he?" he said.

"Yeah," Moe replied, laughing with him. "Like there really is any innocent people in this asshole of a town."

Will and Gid were halfway back to their own office when Muley caught up with them.

"Marshal! It's the Tuckers and the McAfees," he said, excitedly. "They're down at the corral waitin' for you."

"Waiting for us?" Gid asked, the inflection of his voice showing that he was confused by the remark.

Muley nodded. "They're wantin' to shoot it out with you," he said.

"Are they now?" Will replied.

Muley nodded. "Yes, sir. And Deputy Gentry? He's with them too."

Gid grinned, broadly. "Gentry too? Well, what do you know, Will?" he said. "We must've been livin' right. Christmas is comin' early this year."

Will and Gid pulled their guns and checked the loads, then replaced them loosely in the holsters.

"A shootout!" Muley shouted then, running down the street. "The Crocketts, the Tuckers and the McAfees are goin' to shoot it out!"

Muley's shouts were picked up by others, so that soon, people were pouring out into the street from all the stores and houses.

One of those who came outside didn't do so just to watch. Doc Hawkins came to join in, and he moved out into the middle of the street to walk alongside Will and Gid.

"Doc, this isn't your fight," Will said.

Doc looked hurt, as if the Crocketts were going to dinner and he hadn't been invited.

"That's a hell of a thing for you to say to me," Doc replied. "Are you telling me you don't want my help?"

Will looked at Doc, who was nattily dressed as always. "All right," he said. "Raise your right hand."

Doc did so.

"You're deputized," Will said.

"A lawman," Doc said with a little laugh. "This could be the start of a whole new career." Doc broke out into a spasm of coughing.

"You all right, Doc?" Gid asked.

"Don't you worry about me," Doc replied. "I'll be right here with you."

Chapter Twenty-Two

Two of those in the growing crowd were Polly Carpenter and Lucy Briggs. As the Carnation House was close to the Jingle Bob Corral, it was an easy walk over to a place that gave them a front-row vantage point to the action that was about to take place.

"Lenny, no!" Lucy shouted when she saw him standing there with his brother and the others. "Lenny, you don't belong there! You're not like them! Leave! If they're crazy enough to get themselves killed, let them!"

Lenny heard Lucy's anguished shout and looked over at her with an expression of such finality that it was as if he were already dead.

Polly looked at Lenny and the others, then looked down the street toward the three men who were walking, resolutely, toward this rendezvous with destiny. She couldn't see one ounce of emotion in the faces of any of the three. When she looked back toward the five they would be facing, though, she could read their thoughts quite easily. Lenny's face showed resignation, while Moe's and the McAfees' reflected fear and excitement. The foolish bravado of Moe and the McAfees would be no match for the cool courage of the Crocketts, Polly thought. Roscoe Gentry who was standing with them, showed only fear.

Sheriff Jones suddenly appeared, stepping out into the street. He held his hand up to stop Will and the other two.

"Look, boys, we've had our differences," he said. "But this is no way to handle it."

"Sheriff, they're the ones who sent word to settle it," Will replied. "I figure if it doesn't happen now, while we're facing them, it could happen later when we're not looking."

"Gentry is with them," Gid said.

"That's what I mean. Gentry is my responsibility."

"You're welcome to throw in with us, Sheriff," Doc suggested.

Jones looked at the three men for a moment, then, shaking his head, he stepped back out of the street. "No," he said. "You boys are on your own now. I wash my hands of it."

Doc chuckled. "Why not?" he asked. "It worked for Pontius Pilate."

For a moment, Polly had harbored the irrational

thought that perhaps Sheriff Jones could stop the fight. Now she knew with certainty that it was going to take place. Nothing on earth could stop the killing that was about to happen, and she felt her heart go to her throat. She raised her hand to her mouth and watched, numbed with fear.

"Polly, Lenny is going to be killed," Lucy said in a frightened voice.

Polly put her arm around Lucy by way of answering.

By the time Will, Gid and Doc had drawn even with Polly, their adversaries—Lenny, Moe, the two McAfees and Deputy Gentry—stepped out in front of the barn, in a little open lot.

Finally, the two parties of men faced each other, standing no more than ten feet apart. The Tuckers, the McAfees, and Gentry were now boxed in, for the Crocketts and Doc were standing in the open place toward the street. A house blocked one side and a boot repair shop the other. Only the open door of the barn behind them offered any means of escape.

There was a moment of silence as the men confronted each other. Then Will spoke.

"All right, Moe, this is your party," he said. "We're going to give you the first dance."

Isaac McAfee made the first move. "You son of a bitch!" he shouted as he reached for his .45.

"No!" Gentry suddenly shouted, throwing his gun down. He took a couple of hesitant steps backward. "No, wait! We'll be killed!" Gentry turned and ran through the open door of the barn behind them. "No, don't shoot us, don't shoot us!" he begged.

"Gentry, you lily-livered coward!" Lenny shouted.

Polly saw Lenny aim at Will, holding his gun at arm's length. There was something unreal about it, as if she were watching a drama on stage. But Will, who was the most skilled of all of them, had his gun out as quickly as any of them, and the first shot came from Will's gun.

Despite the fact that Lenny was aiming at Will, Will concentrated his aim on Moe, for Moe was known to be the best shot of the four remaining men. Polly heard the boom and saw the recoil kick Will's hand up, and she saw the great puff of smoke from the discharge. She heard Moe call out in pain, then she saw him grab his stomach as blood spilled between his fingers. Moe went down. At the same time that Will shot Moe, Gid shot Amos, hitting him in the chest. Lenny fired at Will but missed.

After that, guns began to roar in rapid succession. The next person to be hit was Lenny. A bullet from Doc's pistol tore through Lenny's right hand. Another hit him in the chest.

"Lenny!" Lucy screamed.

Lenny staggered back against a window of the vacant

house, then slid slowly to the ground. He switched his pistol to his left hand. Sitting there on the ground with his legs crossed, resting his pistol on his shattered arm, he shot with his left hand. His bullet caught Doc between the eyes and Doc went down. Gid shot Lenny again, this time in the lower ribs.

"Lenny, oh my God!" Susie cried.

Out of the corner of her eye, Polly could see Gentry running toward the railroad track.

Isaac McAfee was the only challenger left standing and he drew blood from Gid, hitting him in the left shoulder. Gid and Will both returned fire at the same time and their bullets slammed into his chest. Isaac stumbled out into the street and lurched over toward the people who had crowded around to watch. Unable to shoot for fear of hitting someone in the crowd, Will and Gid both held their fire.

Isaac grabbed onto the post which supported the roof over the boot repair shop. Polly and Lucy were standing on that same porch so that, for a moment, Polly was close enough to him to reach out and touch him. Inexplicably, Isaac smiled at her before he fell back, dead in the dirt.

Now, only Lenny was left alive. He had been knocked flat on his back by Will's last shot, but he managed to work himself upright again. He aimed his pistol at Will and pulled the trigger. The hammer fell on an empty cylinder.

Lenny kept pulling the trigger over and over again, but by now the last shot of the fight had been fired, and there remained only the echoes from the distant hills, and the *click, click, click* of metal on metal as the hammer of Lenny's gun kept falling on empty chambers.

Will stood there watching Lenny as he worked the gun. Of all those who had begun the fight, only Will was still standing unscathed. Gid was wounded and Doc was dead. Moe Tucker and Isaac and Amos McAfee were dead, and Lenny was dying.

"Give it up, Lenny," Will said quietly.

Now that the gunfire had died, Lucy jumped down from the porch of the boot repair shop and ran over to Lenny. She got down on her knees beside him and took his gun from him.

"One more shot, God," Lenny said. "Please, one more shot."

"Lenny!" Lucy cried. "Oh, Lenny, why did you do this? You've always managed to stay out of trouble. Why, now, of all times, did you join with them?"

"I had no choice," Lenny answered in a labored voice. "I had to be loyal to my brother."

Polly had come part of the way with Lucy, and she heard Lenny's words. Suddenly she remembered the conversation she once had with Will about loyalty and she turned to look at him. Will had already put his gun away and was just standing there, looking at Lenny with the saddest expression she had ever seen in a man's face.

"Will," Lenny called.

Will moved forward. "Yes, Lenny?"

"I hope you understand," he said. "We do what we have to do."

"I know," Will said.

Lenny took a couple of audible gasps, then the light faded from his eyes.

"No!" Lucy called. "No, Lenny, no!"

Lucy cradled Lenny's head in her lap and looked up as the townspeople approached. The fight had been witnessed by scores of people and now Polly could see them looking down at the bodies of the slain, at Lucy, and even at her. None of the townspeople said anything. Their looks weren't of pity, or compassion, or even hate. Most were of morbid curiosity as if they were experiencing a sensual pleasure from being so close to death while avoiding it themselves.

"Did you ever see anythin' like this?" someone asked.

"Never," another answered. "Did you see ol' Gentry skedaddle? I never seen such a coward."

"It was over in a hurry, wasn't it?" someone asked.

"Thirty-seven seconds," another said, holding a watch in his hand. "I timed it."

Will looked over at Gid, who had stuffed a handkerchief into the bullet hole. "You all right?" he asked.

"Not much to it," Gid answered. "Doc didn't fare so well though."

"Dead?"

"Yeah."

"It's shame," Will said. "He was good man."

Gid started reloading his pistol. "Come on, Big Brother," he said. "We've got one more to go."

"Did you see where he went?"

"You talking about Gentry?" Henry Deer asked.

"Damn, Henry, if you're down here, who's minding the bar?" Will asked.

"Don't need anyone," Henry answered, taking in the crowd with a wave of his hand. "Everyone is down here."

"Yeah, we are talking about Gentry," Will said. "Did you see where he went?"

"He ran across the tracks over into the Mexican side of town," Henry answered.

When Will, Gid, and Henry crossed the tracks and started down into the *barrio*, they saw a crowd of people gathered in front of the cantina. They were all in one large circle and they seemed to be looking at something.

"What do you think that is?" Gid asked, pointing toward the crowd.

"I don't know," Will answered. "I just hope that whatever it is, it wasn't such a distraction that no one saw Gentry. I'd hate for the son of a bitch to get away now."

"I don't think we're going to have to worry about him getting away," Gid replied. He pointed to what was holding the attention of those who had gathered here.

Deputy Roscoe Gentry was standing in the middle of the street in front of the Nugget de Plata Cantina. He wasn't alone; he had his arm around the neck of a *puta de la cantina* and he was holding a knife to the terrified bar girl's throat.

"Did you ... did you kill them all?" Gentry asked.

"No," Will said. "One is still alive. For now."

"Who? Who didn't you kill?"

"You, Gentry," Will said. "We haven't killed you, yet."

"Get away," Gentry said. "Get away or I'll kill the whore."

"Like you killed Marie?" Gid asked.

"What makes you think I killed her?"

"There was only one knife like hers in town, and now you're holding it."

"She had it coming," Gentry said. "She was always acting so high and mighty around everyone like she wasn't a whore. She wouldn't give me the time of day."

"I'll be damn," Gid said. "I was making a wild guess. Now that I know you killed her; I'm going to enjoy killing you even more than I thought."

Both Will and Gid raised their pistols and aimed at Gentry.

"Don't you fools understand? I'll kill this ..."

Whatever Gentry was going to say was interrupted by the sound of two shots being fired simultaneously. One of the bullets hit Gentry in the gun hand, so that he was unable to pull the trigger. The other shot found that sliver of Gentry's head that he was showing around the girl.

The girl screamed in shock and fear as the two bullets whizzed by so close then she was silent as she realized that there was no more threat. The man who was holding the gun against her was now dead.

With a little cry of relief, the girl ran back into the cantina.

"You have sent him to hell, *Señor*," one of the Mexican bystanders said.

"I expect we have," Gid said.

By now dozens of residents of the Mexican quarter had been drawn to the scene. There, lying belly-up on the ground in front of the cantina, was Deputy Roscoe Gentry. There was a bullet hole just above his right eye, and flies were already swarming around the blood that had oozed from the wound to spread out on the dirt around him.

Will took off his star and dropped it on the ground alongside Gentry's body. Gid did the same thing, then the two brothers turned, and walked away.

When Gid and Will dropped by Carnation House all the girls were gathered in the parlor.

"Lucy, we're sorry about Lenny," Will said.

"You had no choice, I understand," Lucy replied.

"Polly, we've come to say goodbye," Gid said.

"Where will you go?" Polly asked.

"I don't know," Will answered.

"What do you mean you don't know? You can't just go somewhere if you don't know where you're going."

"Polly, when you left Memphis, was it in your mind that you were coming to Shafter to run a bordello?"

"No, when I left home, I had no intention of ever managing a whorehouse. This just sort of happened and ..." Polly interrupted her sentence with a smile. "Yes, I guess I can see what you're talking about."

"I thought you would."

"I'll never see either one of you again, will I?"

"Never is a long time," Gid said.

With a tip of their hats to Polly and the girls, Gid and Will left.

"If only I had met one of them before I got into this ... business," one of the girls said.

"It wouldn't have mattered," Polly said. "They aren't real, not in the way of any man you've ever known. They are phantoms; they are dust in the wind."

"Maybe we should have stayed for a while," Gid suggested.

"Why, little brother?"

"Yeah," Gid replied. "Why should we?"

A Look At: Law of the Rope (The Crocketts' Western Saga: Three)

Non-stop action through the western frontier!

After rescuing Pamela Wellington from varmints, Will and Gid escort her to her daddy's spread – Camelot, a bright, shining 60,000-acre kingdom in the middle of Texas. But like that golden ranch of yore, there's a foul-smelling evil afoot. And it's not Gid Crockett's boots.

AVAILABLE SEPTEMBER 2021

About the Author

Robert Vaughan sold his first book when he was 19. That was 57 years and nearly 500 books ago. He wrote the novelization for the mini-series Andersonville. Vaughan wrote, produced, and appeared in the History Channel documentary Vietnam Homecoming.

His books have hit the NYT bestseller list seven times. He has won the Spur Award, the PORGIE Award (Best Paperback Original), the Western Fictioneers Lifetime Achievement Award, received the Readwest President's Award for Excellence in Western Fiction, is a member of the American Writers Hall of Fame and is a Pulitzer Prize nominee.

Vaughan is also a retired army officer, helicopter pilot with three tours in Vietnam. And received the Distinguished Flying Cross, the Purple Heart, The Bronze Star with three oak leaf clusters, the Air Medal for valor with 35 oak leaf clusters, the Army Commendation Medal, the Meritorious Service Medal, and the Vietnamese Cross of Gallantry.